Nikki vs Jess

United Against the World

Liezl Shnookal

Publisher: Inspiring Publishers,
P.O. Box 159, Calwell, ACT Australia 2905
Email: publishaspg@gmail.com
http://www.inspiringpublishers.com

 A catalogue record for this
book is available from the
National Library of Australia

National Library of Australia The Prepublication Data Service

Author: Liezl Shnookal
Title: Nikki vs Jess
Genre: Modern Contemporary Fiction

Paperback ISBN: 978-1-922920-96-6
ePub2 ISBN: 978-1-922920-97-3
PDF eBook ISBN: 978-1-922920-98-0

CONTENTS

This book is dedicated to my truly remarkable friend, Julie Gillespie. Without her, there would be no Nikki and I would have no story to tell. Together, Julie and I make a wonderful team.

LATE
(Jess)

Sprinting across the quadrangle at TAFE, I flew past a couple of students I knew.

'Sorry, can't stop!' I yelled over my shoulder. 'In a hurry!'

Racing into the Perry building, I rushed down a flight of stairs and flung open the door to the female toilets. The place was completely deserted.

'Bugger!' I said aloud, the word echoing off the tiled walls.

I threw my backpack onto the floor and hoisted myself up to sit on the washbasin ledge so that I could catch my breath. Suddenly a voice came from the far end.

'Where the hell have you been?'

I smiled with relief. I'd failed to see that there was an occupied cubicle.

'Sorry.'

'Is it 1990 yet?'

'Don't be so melodramatic,' I replied. 'I'm only five minutes late.'

There was the sound of flushing and my friend Nikki stomped out of the cubicle, tucking in her flannelette shirt and doing up her bib and brace overalls. Scowling, she stopped to eyeball me.

'Why do you bother to wear a watch when you don't give a shit about the time?'

'My dear,' I replied, assuming a fake wavery voice, 'please don't be cross. I know I'm late, but you have to make allowances for us old folk. We aren't as spry as we used to be.' Because I'm four years older, Nikki likes to refer to me as a senior citizen even though I've only recently had my twenty-first birthday.

Nikki turned away to hide her smile and began scrubbing her hands with a small nail brush. I groaned inwardly. As my friend is doing a preparatory trades course, her hands are always filthy and I knew from past experience that this procedure can take an extraordinarily long time.

'Can you make it snappy? If we don't leave soon, we won't be able to fit in a game.'

'And whose fault will that be?'

However she did rinse her hands and turn off the tap, before carefully putting the nail brush away in her bag.

'Please hurry,' I begged as she thumped the dryer on.

'What?'

I waited until the dryer had switched itself off and peace had descended.

'Are you ready? Can we head off now?'

Nikki swivelled around to face me.

'Prepare to do battle, Jess! Your winning streak is OVER!' she shouted, before running out of the room.

I immediately leapt off the washbasin ledge and grabbed my backpack, but when I reached the stairwell, the slam of the exit door told me that Nikki had already left the building.

We made it in record time to The Purple Crush, our local pool hall, as both sets of traffic lights were in our favour. The minute we arrived, I selected the pool cues and set up the balls on the table, as I always do, while Nikki collected the drinks – her usual can of Coke and a coffee for me.

It was my turn to break, so Nikki took a seat on a nearby lounge chair. I watched the balls scatter, and then examined the position of each ball on the table. I chose one, took aim and wham! It was a perfect hit, even if I say so myself, with the ball falling neatly into a pocket. Another followed. I sank three balls in a row, before sending the ball too far to the right in my fourth shot.

'Damn,' I muttered and then walked over to Nikki, who was busy chatting up some guy.

'Hey, Nikki,' I said. 'It's your turn!'

ALMOST
(Nikki)

Hurray! Finally it was my turn! I sprang out of the chair and grabbed my pool cue. I decided to go for the ball closest to the top-left hand corner, hitting it in just the right spot. I watched it roll straight towards the pocket. I held my breath but it was going slowly, way too slowly. It stopped short. I smacked my forehead with the palm of my hand and skulked back to my seat.

Jess instantly returned to the table with her cue. Although she hadn't taken her eyes off the game while I'd been playing, she still needed to consider every single option.

'We don't have all bloody day!' I reminded her.

She lowered her body down on the table, set up her angle, readjusted and eventually shot. And pocketed. Then there was another long examination of the balls' positions. That turn Jess sank three more balls, but it took forever. In the meantime, I drank another Coke and threw out all the useless junk in my wallet.

At last it was my go again. The first ball I chose was a straightforward shot, and amazingly I pocketed a second. Yes! I lined up the next ball. It hit the side of the table, before ricocheting into the opposite pocket. I was catching up to Jess! I was on fire! My ball was very close to the black, so I knew that I had to be careful. I positioned the cue and then hit . . . and totally missed the ball. It didn't move, not even a centimetre.

Jess dropped her remaining ball into a pocket, of course, and just as easily, potted the black. She walked over to me, smirking.

'Now what were you saying about my winning streak?'

'One day, I swear, I WILL beat you!' I told her. 'And I'm going to really enjoy wiping that smile off your smug little face and . . .'

'Hey,' Jess interrupted, looking at her watch. 'We don't have time to chat. We have to go!'

As we rushed back to TAFE, I tried to remember what I'd told the teacher the Tuesday before, because I didn't want to use the same excuse for being late two weeks in a row. I decided on the dying grandmother, which is one of my all-time favourites, although it hadn't had a spin around the block for a while. And who knows? Maybe, if I said it often enough, this wish may even come true!

PERHAPS?
(Jess)

The following week, I had to cancel our usual game of pool.

'No, Nikki, I can't play today,' I told her, for the third time.

'Come on! Please,' she wheedled.

'I've already explained to you that my arm is incredibly sore. It must have been the nurse's first day on the job at the blood bank yesterday.'

'Then what about a game later in the week?'

I have absolutely no idea why Nikki is always so desperate to play pool, when she loses every single time. However I do know how persistent she can be, so I agreed to a game on Friday while steering her towards the cafeteria in the meantime.

The place was jam-packed, with hundreds of students all talking at once and a very long queue for the food counter. As we took our place in the line, Nikki began to sing along to an old classic song that was blasting out of some even more antiquated speakers.

'We don't need no education,
We don't need no thought control.'

People started to stare but Nikki didn't care. She belted out the chorus, each time it came around.

'All in all, it's just another brick in the wall,
All in all, you're just another brick in the wall.'

Unfortunately Nikki happens to be tone-deaf and so I was relieved when she stopped singing and switched to playing air guitar. Eventually we arrived at the counter, bought our sandwiches and then managed to find a spare table.

'Oh yuk!' she cried. 'There's something incredibly sticky on this table. No wonder no-one was sitting here.'

'Looks like spilt cappuccino. With sugar.' I wiped my hands on my jeans.

Nikki failed to look impressed.

'What are you two doing here? Isn't this one of your pool days?' asked a deep male voice and Daniel took a seat at our table.

When no reply was forthcoming from either of us, he wisely changed the subject. 'Anyway,' he said, 'I'm glad to see you because I have to buy a car for my cousin. Any recommendations, Nik?'

The two of them launched straight into a debate about the merits and drawbacks of various types of cars, which I only half-followed. Not for the first time, I wondered why Nikki and Daniel hadn't become a couple, given their mutual interest in cars and how well they get along together. However my friend always had her eye on some other guy.

I was just beginning to think about grabbing another coffee, when I became aware that Daniel was leaving.

'I've got a meeting with my CAD teacher, so I'll catch you both later. But thanks, Nik. Good advice about Ford Lasers.'

When we were alone again, Nikki began fiddling with one of her overall straps. I've known her for long enough to recognise this as a sign.

'What's up?'

There was silence.

'I'm waiting.'

'I didn't want to tell you but . . . I've got some news.'

'Good news?'

She nodded.

'Go on.'

'I might have a job. Maybe.'

'Really?'

'My auto teacher knows a motor mechanic who wants to put on an apprentice. He gave me his contact details and told me to apply.'

'And you did?'

'Yeah. I've got an interview this Thursday.'

'Do they know you're female?'

Nikki nodded, grinning nervously.

'That's fantastic!' I shouted. I leapt up to hug her, and then hurriedly sat back down again. 'Maybe we should wait till we hear that you've actually got the job before we get too excited. Remember the last time?'

Nikki's face crumpled and instantly I regretted my words. A month ago, she'd been convinced that she had an apprenticeship, only to have a cousin of the garage owner appear at the very last moment and snatch the job away from her.

'If this one doesn't come through, I don't know what I'll do,' Nikki now wailed.

'Hey, when I said that it's too early to celebrate, I didn't mean that it's time to consider euthanasia.'

'I want the job so much, Jess.' She rested her chin on her hands.

'And hopefully this time, you'll get it.'

She sighed.

'Would you like a drink?' I asked, to distract her.

'I wouldn't mind another can of Coke,' she replied in a small, rather pathetic voice.

'Do you think that you might have a bit of a problem with Coke? What number will this be for the day?'

'So how many coffees have you already had?' she snapped back. 'And while we're at it, how many cigarettes have you smoked today on your road to lung cancer?'

I smiled to myself. I can deal with Nikki much more easily when she's annoyed, than when she's feeling sorry for herself.

After getting our respective poisons, we were on our way back to our table when Nikki began tugging on my arm.

'Don't look now,' she whispered, 'but Gary is sitting over to your left, near the wall.'

I spun around and narrowly missed colliding with two mature-aged students.

'The guy you like? Is he the one in the red shirt?'

'Get serious! No, blue T-shirt. Curly dark hair.'

'Where?'

'Don't stare, Jess!'

'I'm not! I'm just trying to work out which one he is.'

'Over there, near the pot plants.'

'Oh yeah. Not bad. I'd give him a score of 75%. Maybe even 80%.'

'Stop gawking! He's going to see us,' Nikki hissed, pulling so hard on my arm that I almost dropped my coffee.

'Settle down,' I said, 'he's not *that* gorgeous.'

She just raised her eyebrows at me.

Back at the table, I began to tell Nikki about an essay I was writing for my Community Development course. I assumed that she'd be interested, since it was about women's participation in non-traditional trades during the Second World War.

'What? You're worried that your essay is too long?' Nikki exclaimed, completely missing the point. 'You've accidentally written too much? How is that possible?'

'It's an interesting topic and I guess that I overdid the research.'

'Well, I prefer to learn through practical experience,' she scoffed. 'I don't have to write essays to become a motor mech.'

Nikki finished the last mouthful of Coke and managed to land her empty can in a nearby rubbish bin. She can be such a cocky little brat sometimes.

'Library, library, LIBRARY!' I shouted at her.

Nikki snorted. 'I've told you before not to use four-letter words in my presence!'

'Seven letters, to be exact, which you would know if you spent more time inside one. Hey, you might even learn how to spell the word if you opened more than a car manual!'

'Oh. So when am I fixing your rust-bucket of a car?' Nikki asked. 'Sunday week, isn't it? Perhaps that might be a good day for you to start teaching me how to spell?' She narrowed her eyes into two little slits. 'That is, of course, if you honestly believe that the ability to spell is more important than any mere mechanical skill.'

'I've just remembered something,' I said quickly. 'Throughout history, there's been many truly brilliant people who couldn't spell. Albert Einstein, for example.'

'Really?'

'And nowadays it's even less important, because we have computer programmes that automatically correct bad spelling.'

'You little brown-nose!'

'If my nose needs to be brown in order to be mobile again, I can assure you that it's worth it.'

We both laughed.

As it was time for class, we made our way out of the cafeteria. Outside, I turned to face my friend.

'Good luck with the job interview,' I said. 'Here's hoping that this time you get it.'

Nikki grinned at me and waved a pair of crossed fingers in the air, before she marched off in the direction of the trades area.

YES!
(Nikki)

I was extremely nervous during the interview and my hands were shaking so badly that I had to hide them under the table. In the beginning, I could barely speak. Mr Saunders, the owner of the garage, waited for me and eventually I managed to tell him that I wanted the apprenticeship more than anything I'd ever wanted in my life. He nodded then. He studied my resume for a long time, and commented that I'd done a lot of automotive classes at school. He also seemed interested in my preparatory apprenticeship course that I'm now doing at TAFE.

Mr Saunders told me that he'd let me know sometime early next week. I wanted to ask whether that meant Monday or Tuesday but as he was already walking me out the door, I just thanked him and left.

However, it was only a couple of hours later when he rang and told me that I had the job.

'YES!' I bellowed at the top of my lungs, after I'd hung up the phone. I leapt onto my bed, kicking off all the pillows, and began jumping up and down. I imagined pulling engines apart in the garage, with a whole heap of tools at my disposal, and learning how to operate the wheel alignment machine and commercial tuning apparatus. My head permanently under the bonnet of a car, or a chassis. Finally my dream was actually going to come true.

Suddenly the bed made a slight cracking noise, reminding me that I'm no longer the weight of a kid and so I decided to walk into the sitting room to share my news with the parents. As to be expected, they were the exact opposite of enthusiastic.

'You've got an apprenticeship, Nicole? You do know that you'll have to stick at it for four whole years, don't you?'

Go Dad.

'Yes, but it's what I want to do,' I told him, although I wasn't sure why I was bothering.

'You'll have to go to school as part of your apprenticeship. And we all know how much you hate studying, Nikki.'

Go Mum.

'Trade school is different. I enjoy learning when it's about cars.'

My mother turned away from me to face my father. 'Perhaps,' she said, 'in a year's time, they'll move her out of the garage and into the office.'

It was times like these that made me wonder who the hell these two people were, and often they looked at me as if I'd just arrived from another planet. Maybe that's how it always is with adopted children – they never manage to belong with their new family.

I was adopted when I was just a baby, very soon after I'd been born. Apparently, my birth mother was a sixteen-year-old girl who couldn't afford to keep me. My parents couldn't have children of their own and so for ages they'd been on an adoption waiting list. One day, completely out-of-the-blue, they received a call from Matron Robinson and straight away were presented with a baby. Me. Talk about pass the parcel.

So now I'm stuck with these people who pretend to be my parents, and they're none too happy about the situation either. Ever since I got caught stealing lollies from the local shop, the old man has grumbled about 'defective genes' and 'bad blood'. Can there really be good and bad bloodlines for people, like there are for horses? Does this mean that I'm never going to win the Melbourne Cup? I have to admit that it had its funny side.

Yet when I ended up in Juvenile Court at fourteen for joyriding in a stolen car with my boyfriend, nobody even came close to cracking a smile. Dad complained bitterly that it had cost him good money to adopt me. So what did he want – a bloody refund? I explained to him a million times that I didn't know that the car was hot but he never believed me. This made me so angry that I felt like going straight out and pinching a car from right under his very nose.

Anyway, I thought happily to myself, from now on I'll be spending all of my time fixing cars, and getting paid for it! I whistled, and then whistled again. My dog finally appeared from the direction of the kitchen, blinking. He's such a sleepy-head, and always has been. I got him when I was a little kid, on the day that I was diagnosed with measles. The doctor instructed me 'to take Panadol and rest up in bed', which is exactly what I did. Since then, Panadol has never failed to make me feel a whole heap better, whatever the problem, although I do sometimes wish that he didn't leave his dirty pawprints on my doona.

With Panadol now awake and trotting behind me, I went outside and dragged the tarp off the car that I'm fixing, a Ford Falcon XB. The Beast stood there in all his shining glory. When I opened the passenger side door, Panadol jumped in and immediately lay down on the seat. He knew the routine. I got in the other side and decided not to turn on the radio – the last time we'd spent a fair amount of time in the car, we'd flattened the battery. So we sat there in complete silence as darkness fell, while I made a list in my head of all the tools I was going to borrow from the garage. Panadol, of course, entertained himself by snoozing.

The minute Jess saw the expression on my face the next day, she guessed what had happened. She hugged me and began firing questions.

'So when do you start?'

'Monday week.'

'What time?'

'Seven in the morning – now that's going to hurt! But I'll manage.'

'How are you going to get there?'

'Train, unless you want to drop over every day and drive me?'

'In your dreams.'

'Actually, knowing the way you drive, it'd be in my nightmares!'

We both chuckled.

Suddenly Jess looked serious. 'Hang on a minute,' she said. 'Does this mean that I won't be seeing your ugly mug around here anymore?'

'Sorry to disappoint. Because I start so early, I finish around 3 pm so I can drop in here after work, no problem. Also part of my apprenticeship involves going to Trade School, which is just up the road. You're not getting rid of me that easily!' I grinned.

'This is perfect. You get paid for doing what you love, plus you still get to hang out here! What more could you possibly want?'

'To beat you at pool?' I suggested.

'When are you going to give up?'

'WHEN I WIN!'

Jess and I shouldered each other through the door of the toilets and raced up the stairs towards the car park and The Purple Crush.

AN END
(Jess)

As everyone knows, I'm the far superior pool player. That game was simply an aberration. Besides, the ball only just managed to drop in, as if by chance, after teetering on the edge for ages. Nikki was jubilant, of course, even doing a victory dance around the table until I reminded her that in actual fact, she hadn't won the game. Unfortunately losing by only one ball has made her even more determined to beat me and she was begging for a rematch the instant I pocketed the black.

Nevertheless, I was so overjoyed that she'd finally scored an apprenticeship, that I bought her a giant shifter spanner as a present and even had it engraved with her name. Afterwards, I walked around the corner to the real estate agents' office to pay the month's rent for the flat, before heading home. I frowned at my broken-down car parked in the street outside our apartment block. Sunday, when Nikki was coming around to fix it, couldn't arrive soon enough.

The flat I share with my boyfriend Luke is cheap and is located fairly close to TAFE. However, that's the full extent of its charm. It consists of a tiny bedroom, a bathroom which is so cramped that it transforms the removal of clothes before a shower into an acrobatic feat, a mini-kitchen which is dwarfed by a huge fridge (with rarely anything in it) and a lounge room whose chairs are so old that the springs make lounging an experience similar to acupuncture.

It's one of those places where it's possible to carry on a conversation with each other from anywhere within the flat. Its smallness may have provided us with plenty of opportunities to communicate, but it hasn't done much for the health of our relationship. At the moment I try not to be home very often. Usually when I am home, Luke isn't. We have been living together for six months now, and I sometimes wonder if we've become an old married couple, which is actually rather strange, given that we are neither married, nor old.

Yet both Luke and I prefer the flat, humble though it may be, to the chaotic share-houses we've both had the misfortune to experience. Where do all those weird psychotic house-mates come from? How do they know exactly what to do to make your co-existence with them a living hell? And Luke and I agree the flat is also infinitely better than trying to co-habit with our own families. That fate is too awful to even contemplate.

On this particular night, Luke surprised me by being home.

'How was your day? Did you get to pay the rent?'

'Yeah, just made it in time before they shut.'

'That's good because I wasn't going to have time to do it tomorrow.'

See what I mean about an old married couple? Scintillating stuff.

'Jess, we need to talk,' Luke suddenly said, looking serious.

Had I been leaving too many dirty clothes around again? I grabbed the ashtray, sat down on the floor and lit a cigarette.

'Are you happy?' he continued. 'Are you happy with how your life is going at the moment?'

'Compared to the life of a heroin addict, most homeless people and of course all the starving Ethiopians, I'd say that life is currently pretty good for me,' I replied.

But Luke sighed, and rested his head in his hands. I started to feel uneasy.

'What about you, Luke? Are you happy?'

He looked at me gratefully. 'No, not at all.'

'Why? What's wrong?' If he was the one who wanted to talk, why was I helping him so much?

Luke sighed again. I shifted position on the floor and decided to remain silent.

'Jess,' he began cautiously, 'what's our future?'

'Our future?'

'Shouldn't we be making plans, building dreams?' Luke asked.

'But you're twenty-three years old,' I reminded him. 'I'm twenty-one.'

'Exactly.'

We were clearly not on the same wavelength.

'What's the hurry? We've only been living together for a few months. Why are we talking about this now?' I studied Luke's face and wondered why my boyfriend had turned into such a stranger.

'I feel as if I'm drifting. I want to know where I'm going, where we're going as a couple. I want to start making some decisions. I think it's time that we grew up.'

'Grew up? Don't you mean – settle down?'

I was becoming annoyed.

'Do you want to start saving for a mortgage on a house?' I continued. 'Perhaps we need to open a joint bank account? Do you want to have kids immediately, or will you be okay if we just buy a dog this year and wait to start our nuclear family a bit later?'

'What are you talking about? And why are you angry?'

'You don't want kids, marriage, a home, superannuation?' I sneered.

'Well, what's wrong with that?'

Appalled, I looked at this stranger who had been sharing my bed for almost a year. Had we had anything in common?

'Jess?'

'Right now I want to finish my Community Development course, and then find a job in that field. At some stage I want to travel. This is what I want.'

'And me? Where do I fit in?' Luke asked.

'Sitting beside me on the bus while we travel together through South America?'

He stared at me. And then, very slowly, and very definitely, he shook his head. Silence deepened around us.

Luke and I had always suspected that there were major differences between us, but we'd comforted ourselves with that little homily that 'opposites attract'. But now that we had laid bare our differences, a massive chasm seemed to have opened up between us.

Eventually Luke got out of his chair and came over to where I was sitting cross-legged on the floor. He looked sadly down into my face.

'I'm sorry, Jess,' he whispered.

He reached down and gently kissed me on the cheek, before disappearing into the bedroom. In that moment, we both realised that our relationship was over.

For ages I just sat there, in shock. I noticed that tears were welling up in my eyes, which I quickly blinked away. I'm no cry-baby and besides, what's the point of blubbering? It never makes me feel any better, or actually helps.

'Damn,' I said aloud, realising that I should have put the shifter spanner on visa instead of paying cash for it. From past experience I knew that moving house was extremely expensive. I lit a cigarette, inhaled deeply and then groaned. Moving was one thing, but there was an even greater problem that lay ahead. Where the hell was I going to live now?

A BEGINNING
(Nikki)

I stared at the shifter spanner that Jess had just given me.

'Do you like it?'

'Er, it's good!'

And it was, kind of. I didn't want to tell her that it was very poor quality and was probably going to bust the minute I used it. Luckily I had an idea.

'You know what, Jess? I'm going to hang it on my bedroom wall, that way it's going to last forever,' I said, as we walked over to the cafeteria.

Daniel was there before us and so we joined him at his table.

'Nikki's got a Motor Mech apprenticeship!' Jess announced, the instant we'd sat down.

'That's fantastic! Congratulations!' Daniel patted me a few times on the shoulder.

I felt like royalty, or that I'd won Tattslotto. At last something totally great had happened to me.

'It's with Saunders Motors,' I told him. Daniel is a bit of a petrol head himself, so I knew he'd be interested in the details. 'It's a small place, with the owner plus a couple of other motor mechs. It's only the second time they've taken on an apprentice. And you should see the tools they have!'

'Yeah?' Daniel's eyes lit up. He likes tools almost as much as I do. It was such a shame that he was doing a Mechanical Engineering course and not a Motor Mech apprenticeship.

'I won't have to buy anything myself. I'll be able to use all their stuff when I work on my car.'

'What car?' asked Jess. 'You don't have your licence yet.'

'I'm fixing one up for when I do. Haven't you heard of forward-planning?'

'But why waste your time on a Ford Falcon?' interrupted Daniel.

'Yeah, right. A Holden Torana is a much better car!' I scoffed.

Daniel thinks that to finish off his precious Torana, it just needs a wax and a polish. I privately reckon it needs kero and a match.

'What about Mazdas? Are they any good?' asked Chris, a guy who was seated at our table. Chris isn't known for his intelligence.

Neither Daniel nor I bothered to reply.

'Hey,' broke in Jess, 'wasn't Kylie Minogue a motor mechanic?'

I started to sing, *'Neighbours, everybody needs good neighbours . . .'* while Jess rudely covered her ears and begged me to stop.

'But in reality, can girls become motor mechanics?' asked Chris, dubiously.

I was halfway across the table, mid-launch, when Daniel intercepted and pushed me back into my chair.

Meanwhile Jess was asking, very quietly, 'So you're saying that they can't?'

'Who gives a pinch of crap what he's saying!' I muttered under my breath, but Chris was continuing.

'Well,' he said, 'working on cars involves getting incredibly dirty. Girls don't like that sort of thing.'

'Excuse me,' interrupted a voice from behind. We swivelled around to face the speaker who was sitting at a nearby table. 'But would you say that working with grease is more disgusting than working with human excrement?' she asked Chris.

'What?' he stuttered. I wasn't sure if Chris's vocab was so limited that he didn't understand the last word, or if he was thrown by how gorgeous this girl looked. She certainly was a babe.

'Women are often expected to deal with huge amounts of vomit, blood, piss and shit . . . pardon my French, boys,' she paused, and smiled sweetly.

Chris was staring at her, his mouth gaping.

'My sister is doing nursing,' she continued, 'which is considered to be an acceptable career for a girl. I guess society believes that it's okay for a girl to get dirty while she's looking after people, but not okay when she's looking after cars.'

She gave me a little wink and I was just about to speak, when a girl sitting on the other side of Daniel cut in first.

'But what about all that heavy lifting? Girls have to be careful about how much they lift, don't they? I mean, none of us want to do any damage to our, oh, you know, our reproductive system.'

I gave her a look that hopefully withered her precious internal girlie bits, while Jess responded in a calm voice.

'Have you heard that there's a wonderful thing called technology? There are now tools and equipment, which make Arnold Schwarzenegger look-alikes totally redundant. With lots of brains and only a little bit of brawn, women – and even puny guys – can do all sorts of jobs.'

'And it's not considered cool, anymore,' added the beautiful girl, 'to wreck your back, regardless of whether it's a male back or a female one.'

There was silence. We'd definitely won the argument. Jess and I introduced ourselves to the newcomer, who told us that her name was Amanda.

'What?' I exclaimed, puzzled. 'That isn't your real name, is it?'

She shook her head. 'My parents gave me another name, but this is the name I've chosen for myself.'

'How come?'

'Because I'm Australian.'

'You don't look Australian.'

'Well, I am.'

'Where were you born?'

'Vietnam, but I came here when I was five.'

'So you're Vietnamese.'

'No, I've lived in Australia for most of my life.'

To my surprise, Jess suddenly piped up. 'Amanda,' she said. 'I think that you have every right to pick your own name and to choose who you want to be. In fact, I admire your courage.'

I watched them smiling at each other as if they'd been best mates forever, and decided to bail out of the discussion. But frankly, I didn't get it. Obviously Amanda (or whatever-her-name-was) had no idea how lucky she was to have real parents and to know where she came from. If she'd been thrown away by her mother at birth, just as I had, then I don't think that she'd be so keen to reject her background.

Amanda stood up.

'Congratulations on your new job,' she said to me.

'Thanks, and thanks for sticking up for me.'

'Any time. I'm sure it's not going to be the last time you cop some crap.'

'Probably not,' I grinned, 'but I reckon it's also going to be great!'

And actually, it really was. I know it sounds weird, but to head off to the garage in my overalls at 6:30 each morning was my idea of heaven. As I was usually the first one there, I had to wait for Fred Saunders, the head mechanic and owner, to arrive with a key to let me in. Once inside, I'd stand with my back against the big heavy roller doors, breathing in that special smell and looking around the workshop. I always noticed if a tool hadn't been put back properly and would find it so that I could reinstate it on the massive tool board.

Those times in the morning when Fred and I had the garage to ourselves were the best. For when the other guys turned up, I became the 'gopher' – the one who had to go and get the tools for everyone. I even had to collect the lunches. But I didn't complain, as it was just part of what every apprentice was expected to do.

I also didn't make a fuss about the girlie pin-up calendar, not even to Jess. For I knew that she'd be furious and order me to tear the thing off the wall. But there was no way that I wanted to call attention to myself as being any different to the guys. I just wanted to get on with the job, which was exactly what I was doing.

I'M FINE
(Jess)

I didn't mention to Nikki that Luke and I had split up. She would have made it into some earth-shattering catastrophe, which it wasn't. Besides, it wasn't actually any of her business.

Calmly and rationally, Luke and I worked through the logistics of separating. It was obvious to both of us that I had to be the one to move out of the flat, since my income alone wasn't enough to cover the rent. So I scoured the real estate section in the local paper, but quickly came to the realisation that I couldn't afford to rent anywhere on my own. Next I drew up a list of friends in share houses and rang each in turn, only to find that nobody had a spare room. As I crossed the last off the list, I concluded that I had run out of options.

As we all know, desperate times call for desperate measures and for me, this was definitely one of those times. So I hired two men with a van, who took my possessions to a nearby storage place, and I myself moved onto my sister's sofa bed. I then managed to increase my hours where I already worked. This was terrific for two reasons: I was going to be able to afford my own place a whole lot sooner, plus this would be time that I wouldn't have to spend with my sister.

I also began hanging around TAFE a lot more. One day I was passing through the main foyer and stopped to examine the various pamphlets on the Student Union table. Amongst them was a photo, which I picked up in order to have a closer look. A man in a white shirt was standing in front of a line of military tanks, a lone small figure confronting a huge army. The man looked somehow both insignificant and courageous.

'Shocking, isn't it,' said a woman from behind the table.

'Did they run over him?' I asked, although I wasn't actually sure if I wanted to know.

'No, not this particular guy. But the day before, there were countless numbers of people killed by the Chinese army in Tiananmen Square. The students had been protesting there for weeks, calling for democratic reform. They were unarmed; it was a massacre.'

I stared at the photo with increased horror.

'My name's Kym. If you're interested,' continued the woman, 'come along to a meeting at 6:30 pm on Thursday when we'll be talking about solidarity with the Chinese students. The Student Union offices are downstairs, in the basement.'

I'm not sure exactly why I decided to go to the meeting, although I think it was connected to the bravery of the man in the photo. If he could try to block the path of army tanks, putting his own life at risk, then I figured that the very least I could do was to front up to some meeting and see if I could help.

The session was already underway when I arrived, with ten people crammed into a very small office, all arguing with each other. Different kinds of action were heatedly debated in turn but they finally agreed on one of them, after a six-to-two vote. As a newcomer, I abstained. Besides, I didn't fully understand the options. Kym seemed to be a key leader, a firebrand with red hair that exploded out of her head in corkscrew ringlets, and certainly she had the loudest voice. She was very impressive.

When the meeting was over and everyone started to head off, Kym asked if I wanted to stay for a cup of coffee – an offer which I can never refuse.

'Thanks for inviting me to the meeting,' I said, picking the cleanest-looking cup in the sink.

'So what are you studying here?'

'Community Development. And I also do some work as a book-keeper.'

Kym fumbled with a spoon, almost spilling the coffee. 'Really? You do book-keeping?'

'Yes, I did a course in accounting when I finished school.'

'Hey, Dave,' Kym shouted to the guy in the adjoining office. 'Got a moment?'

Dave joined us.

'This is Jess. She's studied accounting.'

They both stared at me for a full thirty seconds, before Dave finally spoke.

'Our Finance Officer has just quit, and we need someone to fill in for the next few weeks. We'll have to advertise the job so it would just be in the interim, but if you're the successful applicant it would be an ongoing job for twelve hours a week.'

'Working for the Student Union?' I asked.

Kym nodded.

Later that evening I walked to the carpark, my head spinning. I had gone to a meeting and been offered a job. I was going to be able to rent my own place even sooner than I had thought. I was back on track.

However, I still had one final bit of damage control left to do. Nikki had rung my old flat and had spoken to Luke.

'What the hell happened?' she cried when we caught up the following Tuesday. 'Why didn't you tell me? Where are you living now? Are you back with your parents?'

'My parents? You've got to be joking,' I said, and stopped. I had never mentioned anything about my parents to Nikki, and was certainly not about to embark on that topic now. 'No, I'm crashing at my sister's place.'

'What? You have a sister?'

I groaned inwardly. I really didn't want to discuss my sister either. It was bad enough that I had to stay there.

'What I don't understand,' I said instead, hoping to shift the conversation onto safer territory, 'is why Luke is so hell-bent on settling down.'

'Yeah, why the rush? It's not like he's turning thirty.'

I turned hurriedly away to hide my irritation. Sometimes I forget how young Nikki is, until she inadvertently reminds me.

'He's so conventional. He wants a wife and kids, plus a white picket fence somewhere out in the suburbs.'

'What's wrong with that?'

I looked at Nikki, shocked. She may be a female apprentice in an all-male trade, but she still held such traditional values. It was all incredibly disappointing.

'Not everyone wants that kind of life. I don't think I do,' I replied.

'Then Luke was the wrong guy for you. You're better off with someone else. Don't worry, he'll come along.'

Was Nikki referring to a 'Mr Right'? Was there really such a person and was it truly that simple? Even if a guy did seem 'right' at the time, where was the guarantee that it was going to work out forever? It didn't for my parents. And besides, did I actually want a boyfriend? Suddenly my choice was 100% clear.

'I don't want a boyfriend. I'm perfectly fine without one,' I said firmly.

Nikki opened her mouth to speak but I cut in quickly.

'Do you want to play pool today, or not?'

'Is the Pope a Catholic?'

We immediately left the toilets, heading towards the car park and The Purple Crush.

TRYING TO KICK-START MY LIFE WITH NO JUMPER LEADS
(Nikki)

I swallowed another mouthful of Coke and stared in amazement at Jess as she chalked her pool cue. She was behaving exactly as she always did. I know that if I was the one who'd been dumped, I'd be an absolute basket-case.

I sighed, wondering why nothing ever seemed to work out for anyone. It clearly didn't for Jess and Luke, and it certainly never did for me either. I had hoped to get my driver's licence the day after I turned eighteen, but this was clearly not going to happen. Both of my parents had refused to take me out for driving practice and honestly, I'd been stupid to have expected anything different.

'It's your turn, Nikki.'

Jess's voice made me jump. I checked out the table and worked out that she must have sunk three balls.

'Who taught you to drive?' I asked.

'My mother, of course.'

'Of course?'

'Well, it definitely wasn't going to be my father.'

Lucky Jess to have two parents, both real parents, who differ. The parents I'm stuck with just seem to take the opposite side to me. And Jess has a sister as well. A whole family, a normal family. Not dysfunctional and adopted, like mine.

'Are you going to play or not?'

I chose the ball closest to the bottom right-hand corner. It spun off the side and missed the pocket by a kilometre. I watched as Jess carefully studied the table and took her shot. As always, she scored.

'Where does your sister live?' I asked.

She glared at me and then snapped, 'Will you please shut up. I can't concentrate with you yabbering all the time.'

I went and sat down. I hate the way Jess gets so grumpy when anyone talks during a game of pool. I wondered if I had a sister somewhere out there in the world, and whether she was as grumpy as Jess. I thought about my real parents, and how they would've helped me get my licence. Parents do that sort of thing for their own flesh and blood, because it's natural to want to look after their biological offspring. That's the way it is with all species. My real parents wouldn't want me to stay stuck forever in the nest, always underfoot. Nothing would've been too much trouble for them. Who knows, maybe my father worked as a car mechanic and would be thrilled that I was following in his footsteps.

'Your go,' Jess said, cutting across my thoughts.

I stood up to inspect what was left on the table and decided to go for the ball in the middle.

'Are you honestly okay without Luke?' I asked.

'Yes.'

The ball dropped beautifully into the pocket.

'Do you miss him?'

I wasn't sure which to try next.

'No. I'm far too clever to waste my time pining after a failed relationship. Besides,' she laughed, 'it's not as if it's the first time that I've broken up with a boyfriend. This happens to be relationship failure number three.'

I chose a ball, although I knew it was a tricky shot.

'In actual fact,' she continued, 'I'm enjoying the freedom.'

I hit, and missed. Sitting back down again, I decided that I wanted to be as independent as Jess. But to be independent, I knew that I needed a driving licence.

Perhaps having an older boyfriend was my answer, just in the short term, because he could take me out driving. Gary? I discounted him immediately. Now that we were both at Trade School together, he was friendly only when nobody else was around. It seemed like he was ashamed to be seen talking to me and so lately I'd begun to wish that our days at Trade School didn't coincide. No, Gary was definitely not an option.

'Should I call for an ambulance?' Jess asked, coming over.

'Huh?'

'I just slaughtered you and you haven't even noticed.'

'Very funny. I happen to have a lot on my mind.'

'Don't do yourself an injury. So can we go now?'

I jumped up and sang, *'We've got to get out of this place. If it's the last thing we ever do,'* as we made our way past the empty pool tables.

At the door, Jess belted out, *'Girl, there's a better life for me and you!'*

'I bloody well hope so!' I snorted in reply.

Arriving back at TAFE, we ran into Daniel.

'Hey, didn't you get your licence a little while ago? Who took you out for driving practice?' I asked.

'Initially it was Dad, but we kept arguing. It was an utter disaster. Then Mum tried to teach me . . .'

'Your mother,' I sighed.

'That was no good either. She gave me a whole lot of wrong advice, so I failed the test the first time around. Finally I paid for some lessons from a proper instructor, which was heaps better.'

'Ha!' I said, grinning at Daniel. 'Why hadn't I thought of that? Thanks!'

My driving instructor's car was an Astra, which was in an even worse condition than Jess's Colt. The instant I jumped in for my first driving session, I realised that it wasn't roadworthy – the windscreen alone would have copped a yellow canary. I opened my mouth to tell him, but luckily changed my mind. Guys seem to think that there's a genetic link between the Y chromosome and metal, and won't listen to any advice about their cars that comes from a female. So I just concentrated on practising my driving technique and said nothing. I wasn't going to let anything, or anyone, stop me from getting my licence.

TAKING OVER THE STREETS
(Jess)

The tram lurched slowly away from the stop as the rain pelted down. A new lot of sodden passengers shook water from their umbrellas, before taking their seats. I tried not to feel too dispirited. Kym from the Student Union office had told me that there was never a good turn-up at rallies when it was wet.

But within fifteen minutes, the sun was intermittently breaking through the clouds. I looked around at the other passengers, trying to assess who cared about peace, and who didn't. I decided it was a 15% to 85% split. However, when the tram veered off in an unexpected direction, presumably re-routed on account of the demonstration, I was surprised to see 70% of all the passengers immediately leap to their feet, eager to disembark. Happily I joined the large mob as we stepped off the tram into sunshine, to make our way towards Parliament House.

Even though the rally wasn't due to start for a little while, there was already a massive crowd gathered at the Bourke St/Spring St intersection. I had never seen so many people in one place, or so diverse. There were conservatively dressed men and women holding up posters against uranium mining; long-haired hippies and ferals exuding a strong smell of patchouli oil; Kurdish family groups; elderly couples holding hands; parents pushing strollers with plastic covers flapping from the handlebars; African youths and white middle-aged men beating drums; roving packs of swaggering teenagers in jeans; yuppies in expensive raincoats wheeling even more expensive bikes; and the Socialists circulating through the crowd as they tried to sell their newspapers.

I scanned the multitude of people but saw no familiar face, realising that it had been idiotic to make arrangements with Nikki to meet on the steps of Parliament House – everyone had made exactly the same plan.

I managed to squeeze through the throng to find a vacant space about halfway up and sat down to properly survey the scene. Colourful banners fanned out in the breeze and placards bobbed up and down. Everyone was talking and laughing together, and there was a definite mood of excitement. I wished that I had thought ahead and made my own poster, like so many others had done. While I sat there, various leaflets were thrust into my hand, which I began to read.

'HEY JESS!' I heard someone yell.

I looked around and to my amazement located Nikki, who was wildly waving her arms a few levels below me. Daniel was there too, with Amanda standing beside him. I made my way towards them.

'Can you believe this? The crowd's even bigger than for a Collingwood versus Carlton footy match!' Nikki exclaimed.

'Of course it is,' I said, 'because it's much more important.'

Nikki opened her mouth to reply when there was a terrible high-pitched ringing noise emanating through a megaphone. Several people rushed to help the man in the suit who was grappling with it, yet the piercing sound persisted so long as the megaphone was switched on. The organisers gave up and signalled to begin the march, so within minutes, everybody began to move. Our little group linked arms as we swept right into the middle of the road, part of a crush of people. There we all were, walking through the city, with not a car or a tram in sight. The streets belonged to us!

Amanda suddenly separated herself from us.

'What's wrong?' asked Daniel.

'Why isn't there a law against smoking?' Amanda complained, fanning her face with a bunch of leaflets.

I feigned deafness.

'Have you been in a coma lately?' Nikki answered. 'There are laws. For example, these days you're not allowed to smoke on domestic flights.'

'I'm talking about a law that controls public places,' Amanda continued to whine. 'It's terrible that people can still smoke in a crowd like this.'

'But we're outside, so what's the problem?'

I was so shocked that I stumbled over a tram track. Nikki on the side of smokers? However, as if right on cue, someone in front of us lit a cigarette and the smoke naturally headed straight towards Amanda's face. A direct hit.

'I see what you mean,' reneged Nikki.

'Me too,' said Daniel.

Amanda doubled the rate of her sanctimonious fanning, frowning her disgust at another smoker. We walked on in silence for a few minutes, while I struggled with my thoughts. Amanda's lack of perspective had infuriated me.

'Do you realise,' I finally said, 'that in some countries, people are actually killed when they attend a demonstration?'

'So?' Amanda asked warily.

'When Chinese demonstrators risk being run over by army tanks or shot, doesn't struggling against the fumes of a cigarette in Australia seem fairly minor by comparison?'

'But we don't live in China.'

'Nevertheless, isn't it reassuring to think that the greatest threat we face in attending a rally in Australia is the risk of passive smoking?'

'The thought of cancer isn't what I'd call reassuring. I'd rather die an instant death than die slowly and painfully in ten years' time.'

'That's ridiculous. The percentage of people who contract cancer from passive smoking is tiny.'

'How tiny?' she asked.

Shit. I'd backed myself into a corner.

'Less than 1%,' I managed, but without much conviction. I hate being vague when it comes to numbers.

'You have the same chance as winning Tattslotto,' came a voice from behind. 'About one in eight million.' I turned to see a silver-haired old woman, who winked at me as she took another drag of her cigarette.

'What wonderful mathematical accuracy,' muttered Amanda.

'Probably a retired maths teacher,' Daniel said, nodding, clearly unaware that she was being sarcastic.

'How many more kilometres are there still to go?' Nikki asked. 'I need a Coke. Anyone else up for a drink?'

Amanda and Nikki broke away from the crowd, with Daniel trailing after them, and they joined a long queue outside a 7-Eleven store. Nikki shouted something across to me but at that point, those around me started to chant and I couldn't hear what she said. I waved over my shoulder at my friends; frankly, I was glad to leave them behind.

We only walked for another five minutes before the people in front of me stopped dead. I stood up on my toes to try to find out what the hold-up was, and was whacked in the head by a giant banner.

'Hey, look out,' I shouted.

'Sorry,' one of the pole bearers said, 'I didn't realise that we'd come to a standstill.' He looked at his watch, then back at me, before adding, 'I've got to hand out some leaflets, but my replacement hasn't arrived. You wouldn't be able to carry this pole for a while, would you?'

I examined the banner which had 'Students for Peace' emblazoned on it in large red letters and agreed. As I took my place, I nodded at the guy who was holding the pole at the other end, then suddenly we were off again. I adapted my walking pace to match my counterpart's, glad to be now truly part of the rally.

We arrived at Treasury Gardens, our destination, where thousands of protestors were already sprawled out on the grass. I rested the pole on the ground — either banners were heavier than I'd imagined or else I was not as fit as I'd hoped — and was relieved to see the other pole-bearer doing the same. Somebody was addressing the crowd from the rostrum way in the distance, and even though we weren't particularly far from a large bank of speakers, it was nevertheless difficult to catch what she was saying.

'What's your name?' interrupted my fellow banner-holder, smiling at me.

'Jess.'

'I'm Max. Thanks a lot for helping out.'

I nodded and turned back to face the stage again, craning to hear.

'There's no way I could've managed without you.'

I didn't respond.

'What are you studying?'

'Community Development.' I kept my eyes firmly fixed in the direction of the stage.

'Interesting?'

'Yes.' Why didn't he get the hint? Subtract thirty marks for lacking perception.

'I'm doing Politics and Economics.'

'If you don't mind, I'd like to try to hear what the speaker is saying.'

'Of course. Please forgive my testosterone.' He spun instantly around to face the speakers. Add twenty for being up-front. I glanced at him, noticing that he had beautiful chestnut hair, just like the mane of a horse I used to ride when I was a kid. Add another ten.

I shook my head to dispel these mental detours and returned my concentration to what was being said on the rostrum. There was a refugee from Vietnam with a terrible story to tell about life in a war zone; likewise a Palestinian woman. Various religious leaders also presented compelling reasons for world peace. It was all quite shocking.

Eventually the speeches finished and the crowd began to disperse.

'I'm leaving now. Bye,' I said to Max who was rolling up the banner.

'Thanks again for your help.'

'No problem.' I turned and began to walk away.

'Jess! Just a minute!' I heard him call. 'There's a conference coming up on Social Action, that's being organised by the National Union of Students.'

I retraced my steps. 'Sounds good.'

'It starts at 9:30 am next Saturday at Trades Hall. You pay at the door.'

'How much does it cost?'

'Registration is forty bucks, with student concession. That's for both days.'

'Thanks. I'll be there,' I said, thinking that the conference would help me write an essay on grassroots campaigning. As I left Treasury Gardens, I smiled to myself. I had marched in a demonstration and was about to attend my first conference. My life was finally starting to head somewhere.

However, poor Nikki was not doing as well.

'What's happened?' I asked, when I saw the miserable expression on her face when we next met at TAFE.

'My driving instructor reckons that girls can't be motor mechs.'

'The bastard! So you've stopped the lessons?'

'Of course.'

'Now what? Don't you need to learn how to drive in order to get your licence?'

'No, because I already know!' she snapped. 'And I'm still booked in for the test.'

'Don't you need to practise though?'

Nikki just scowled in reply.

I knew from personal experience that getting one's licence wasn't that easy. Besides, didn't she need a car for the test? Suddenly I realised that Nikki could do with my help.

'If you like,' I said, 'you can drive my car.'

'What?'

'I have my full licence so it would be legal.'

'That'd be fantastic!' yelled Nikki. 'Why didn't I think of you before? I can't believe how stupid I am sometimes!' She slapped her forehead with the palm of her hand, and then added, 'Can we start now?'

Even before I'd agreed, Nikki had jumped off the washbasin ledge and was racing towards the exit door. Having missed out on lunch hours earlier, I insisted that we pick up some food at the caf, where we bumped into Daniel and Amanda, seated cosily together at a table near the door. Nikki announced proudly that she was off for a drive in my car.

'Do you need to borrow these?' Amanda asked, extracting a set of learner driver plates from her bag. 'And would it be okay if we tag along?'

Oops. I'd completely forgotten about the need for L-plates, therefore I had little choice but to nod to both questions. The four of us headed out to the car park and piled into my car. To my surprise, Nikki was an extremely competent driver, needing only minimal guidance from me. I settled back into the passenger seat, letting her get used to my car. We travelled north along Bates Road, with Nikki concentrating hard. She clearly loved driving. However, after we reached Stuart Street, she began to speed up, so I checked the speedometer to find it on 62.

'*Mustang Sally,*' I began to sing, '*guess you better slow that Mustang down.*'

Without taking her eyes off the road, Nikki poked her tongue out at me but did ease her foot off the accelerator pedal a little.

'Sing it to her, girls,' I ordered into the rear vision mirror. '*All you wanna do is ride around, Nikki!*'

'*Ride, Nikki, ride!*' chorused Amanda and Daniel from the back seat.

Suddenly Daniel took up the lead, singing, '*I bought you a brand-new Mustang, it was 1965.*'

Amanda and I started to sway in our seats, clapping in time.

'*Now you come around, signifyin' woman, but you won't, you won't let me ride! Mustang Nikki! Now baby!*' he wailed.

Nikki chuckled and Daniel lowered his voice, *'Now, Mustang Nikki, you better slow that Mustang down!'*

Amanda and I sang in unison, *'We said, Mustang Nikki, you better slow that Mustang down!'*

'You been running all over town, I guess I'll have to put your flat feet back on the ground,' Daniel threatened.

Shocked, Amanda missed a clap, but Daniel was continuing on, regardless.

'One of these early mornings, I'm gonna be wiping those weeping eyes, yeah.'

'But this ain't no Mustang!' interrupted Nikki, in a phoney American voice. 'It's a goddamn Mitsubishi COLT!'

We all laughed.

'Wait a minute,' said Amanda. 'There's something really wrong here.'

'What do you mean?'

'Why is he going to be wiping the woman's "weeping eyes" when it's *her* car and *he's* the one who isn't allowed to ride in it?'

We all looked at Daniel, the guy, but he shrugged his shoulders.

'Maybe it's got something to do with American culture, which we don't understand?' he suggested.

'Ha!' I scoffed. 'More likely it's another example of the same old sexist patriarchal bullshit.'

Daniel squirmed uncomfortably on his seat, pretending to find something extremely interesting to examine outside the car.

All of a sudden Nikki pulled sharply over to the kerb, wound down the window and tooted the horn.

'Hey! Aunty Lil! Over here!' she yelled.

A middle-aged woman who was walking along the pavement turned to stare.

'Lil, it's me!' shouted Nikki again.

The woman walked briskly over to the driver's side of the car.

'I'm driving!' said Nikki, happily stating the obvious, as she slung her elbow nonchalantly out of the window.

'Hi,' I waved, 'don't mind me, I'm just the insignificant accessory to the car – its owner. I'm Jess and you must be . . . Aunty Lil, perhaps?'

She grinned immediately. 'How on earth did you guess? I trust that Nicola is driving well?'

'Extremely well,' I answered. 'A couple more practices and she'll be perfect.'

Nikki beamed. 'And The Beast is almost finished! I only have to adjust the clutch and the timing. Oh, and get him registered.'

'Wonderful. Now tell me, dear, what's happening for your birthday?' asked Aunty Lil.

Nikki immediately dropped her head. 'Nothing, of course,' she muttered.

'What?'

'As always.'

'But this year it's your eighteenth birthday,' Lil said, noticeably annoyed.

'So?'

'Surely this year there'll be a celebration of some kind.'

'Nup. We're going over to Grandma's for supper, same as we always do. Remember, it's her birthday too.'

'Why can't your father celebrate his mother's birthday on a different day, for a change?'

'Yeah, right.'

'I'll ring your mother and Aunt Rose the minute I get home. This year it's *your* special birthday and we're going to celebrate it whether it suits your father or not!'

'I'm sorry,' I interrupted, 'but it's getting late and I've got another class soon.'

'Gotta fly, Aunty Lil. Be seeing you.' Nikki switched on the ignition.

As we headed back down the road, I said, 'That's good news. Sounds as if you're going to get a party, after all.'

Nikki snorted loudly. 'You think that there's a chance that Lil is going to get what she wants over my father's mother? There's absolutely no way that's going to happen!'

'I don't understand.'

'Then let me explain. My mother is the baby of her family, so she always gives in to her big sisters, Aunty Lil and Aunty Rose. Yet as a man, my father of course wins out over my mother. This means that it's really a contest between my two aunties and my father, with my mother totally out of the picture. But then, there's dear old Grandma. She's the one who actually calls the shots, and believe me, when she says "jump" to my father, it's simply a question of how high. Aunty Lil doesn't stand a chance. Nope. As always, on the day we'll be celebrating my grandmother's birthday, not mine.'

'But it's your eighteenth! Doesn't that count for anything?'

'Not when you're adopted, stupid. Birthdays celebrate the day you're born. Get it?' Nikki gave a bitter laugh.

'I'm not sure.'

Amanda and Daniel remained diplomatically quiet in the back.

'Why would my parents want to party on the anniversary of my birth? Hey, they weren't even there!'

'But surely they want to make it a special day for you?'

'Why would they want to do that? It's not as if they're my REAL parents,' she almost yelled.

'Okay, okay.'

I decided to let the subject drop. Nikki was clearly becoming agitated, and I didn't want to risk an accident. We arrived back at TAFE with only four minutes to spare before my class. Amanda got out of the car, grabbed her L-plates and vanished along with Daniel.

'Nikki, we can do some more driving practice, if you'd like,' I said as she handed over my car keys. 'Just name the day.'

'Tomorrow?'

I nodded and watched her slouch off, hands inside her overall pockets.

'What's that? Did I hear you say thanks?' I shouted after her, before sprinting out of the car park, in the direction of my class.

JUST A PIECE OF GARBAGE
(Nikki)

Panting hard from running all the way from Trade School, I collapsed onto the floor.

'At last!' said Jess. 'I was starting to get worried. How come you're so late?'

I couldn't speak.

'Are you okay?'

I shook my head. Jess got off the washbasin ledge to join me on the tiles.

'I'm never going back to Trade School!' I finally managed to tell her.

'Don't be ridiculous. You love that place.'

'Not any more. Those apprentices are dickheads!'

'What's happened now?'

'They chucked me into a skip.'

'So why didn't you jump out?'

'I couldn't!'

'Why not?'

I glared at her.

'Perhaps,' she added, 'you need to start from the beginning.'

I took a deep breath. 'While I was putting the tools away, I noticed that a few of the apprentices were skulking around the workshop, whispering. Suddenly they grabbed me from behind and threw me into an industrial skip, slamming the lid shut. It was pitch-black inside. I was screaming non-stop, trying desperately to escape, but they were laughing like it was the funniest thing in the world. I felt the skip being pushed around and heard the noise of the car hoist being switched on. Somebody shouted "up, up and away" and I knew that the whole skip was being raised. Then another called "good riddance to bad rubbish" before I heard the door bang. I realised that they all must have left.'

'Hurray,' said Jess.

'NO! NOT hurray! I was left in a skip suspended way up in the air, on a goddamn car hoist. I thought I was going to die in there.'

'You don't think that you're being a little melodramatic, Nikki?'

'What? Those arseholes tried to kill me.'

'Hey, I'm sure that wasn't their intention. Those boys are feeling threatened by having a girl in their class. They're angry because you're like a gate-crasher to their exclusive boys-only party!'

'So I should feel sorry for them?' I shouted. 'Are you serious?'

'All I'm saying, Nikki, is that it might help if you see the bigger picture. Maybe then you wouldn't take it all so personally.'

'I'll try to remember that it's not personal when it's ME they're shoving around!'

Jess sighed and then asked, 'So how did you manage to escape?'

'Mason, one of the teachers, came to lock up and heard me yelling.'

'That was lucky.'

'He's such a deadshit! He couldn't stop laughing.'

'You're kidding.'

'He thought it was hilarious.'

'But as the teacher, it's up to him to ensure that everyone gets a fair go,' said Jess, winding up at last. 'It's illegal that you're being given a hard time because you're female. That's discrimination and he can be sacked for that!'

'Ha! Mason believes that if he treats me as special and needing extra attention because I'm a girl, then somehow he's discriminating against me.'

'That's absurd! You should go to the Equal Opportunity Officer.'

Sometimes I think that Jess lives on a totally different planet to the one I'm on.

'Really? There's one at Trade School? Maybe she shares an office with the Easter Rabbit?'

'Oh. Anyway, what can you do? You have to stand up for your rights.'

Clearly Jess had no idea. I glared at her for a minute.

'Yep,' I said, getting up off the floor, 'I'm standing up for my right not to listen to any more crap. I don't want to play pool today, I'm going home,' I told her, before marching out the door.

With a bus nowhere in sight, I decided to walk to the next stop. Those guys are such bastards, I thought as I strode along. I'd always known that a girl has to be tough in order to survive in a non-traditional trade like motor mech, but I hadn't expected the other apprentices to be so disgusting. What the hell did they have against me? All I ever wanted was to fit in and be part of the group. Then, suddenly, it hit me like a ton of bricks. What an absolute moron I'd been. I'm a girl! Of course guys were never going to accept me as one of them!

But on the other side of the fence, I haven't fitted in with girls either. They don't talk about the stuff that interests me, or do the kinds of things I want to do. We just don't have a lot in common. Even at Tech School, the few girls who were there would look at me like I was some kind of weirdo, because I was taking the trade subjects that boys do. Every day I'd eat lunch on my own.

I arrived at the bus stop just as a bus was pulling in, and found a seat at the very back. I sighed, realising that I'd never fitted in anywhere. There was me, and then there was everyone else. I didn't belong in a group of girls, and I didn't belong in a group of guys. I was different, and no matter how hard I tried, that was never going to change. I was a complete social misfit, an outcast, destined to be rejected by everybody forever.

I must have groaned aloud, because the kid sitting next to me turned around to gawk. I clapped my face between my hands, to snap myself out of being such a sad-sack. It worked. Of course I'd go back to Trade School. I had to finish my apprenticeship and anyway, I wasn't going to let those arseholes stop me. I glanced out the window to see that I was only halfway home. The bus was so goddamn slow — another reason why I had to get my driver's licence. With that in my wallet, I knew there'd be no looking back, except through a rear-view mirror. It was going to be a whole new start.

On the morning of my birthday, I leapt out of bed, fed Panadol and ran through the drizzling rain to have breakfast in The Beast. Only one more sleep, I told him as I patted his dashboard. We could hardly wait!

After breakfast, I opened the envelope that had been left on the kitchen sideboard. It was the usual – some cash inside a card. For my twelfth birthday, my parents had given me a sewing machine. Seriously? Me and a sewing machine? Within a week I'd flogged it, and with the money I'd bought a cool ghetto blaster. That was the last present they ever bought me.

My parents have never known what to do about my birthday. Probably all infertile couples find it hard to celebrate the birth of someone else's baby. And anyway, I wasn't like other kids. I didn't want a birthday cake, party hats or the whole happy birthday kind of crap. I simply couldn't get excited about the date that my own mother chucked me away.

I went off to work extra-early. I hadn't mentioned to anyone, not even Fred, that it was my birthday. However, it turned out to be a good day. I was allowed to do a service on a brand-new Ford totally on my own, and discovered that the brakes were faulty. Fred was very impressed, and even the other mechanics congratulated me.

When I arrived home, I found Aunty Lil and her best friend Edna seated at the kitchen table with my mother, all having a cup of tea. I grabbed a Coke and sat down with them, talking about what had happened in the garage. We were soon joined by Aunty Rose and her friend Ruth, and then a little later, by my father when he returned home from work. Suddenly Lil did a drum roll on the table top, before handing me a card. I opened it. Inside was an IOU for a cruise to Fiji. I stared at her in disbelief. Lil and Edna travel a lot, but I'd never before been invited to go with them.

'This is the best present, ever!' I shouted. 'Are you sure you want me to come?'

'This is way too much,' my father said, with a shake of his head but Aunty Lil ignored him.

'We're not going for another two years, so this will give you plenty of time to get a passport, Nikki,' she said.

Aunty Rose loudly cleared her throat to get our attention, before pushing a biggish parcel towards me. Unfortunately, the car seat covers she'd bought for The Beast weren't the right type, but she promised to exchange them. She also gave me the Nirvana cassette that I'd asked for, so at last I had an actual present in my hands. The minute my aunts left, I raced into my bedroom to listen to it.

However, it wasn't long before I looked up to see my mother standing in the doorway, her mouth flapping. Reluctantly, I turned off my Walkman and removed the headphones.

'Are you ready?' she asked.

It was obvious that I wasn't.

'We're leaving for Grandma's immediately. Have you forgotten?'

If only it could be that easy.

'Can I drive?' I asked my mother's back as she walked out.

'Absolutely not!' came my father's voice from down the hallway. 'I want to get there in one piece.'

Thanks for nothing, Dad.

I got off my bed, brushed my hair and went outside to where my parents were waiting for me in the garage. However it took two changes of clothes before I was finally allowed to get into the car. Stupid, really. No matter what I wear, I'm never good enough for old Grandma.

When we arrived, she was waiting on the verandah. I watched my mother load a mountain of presents from the boot of the car into my father's arms.

'John!' my grandmother called, with a little giggle. 'You naughty boy! I told you not to buy me anything!'

Fully laden, my father walked up the steps.

'Happy birthday, Mum,' he said and together they disappeared into the house.

I waited for my mother, who was carefully extracting the cake she'd baked from the back seat of the car, before following her inside. My father and Grandma were discussing a kitchen tap which was dripping and how it was keeping my grandmother awake. So my father puffed out his not-so-hairy chest and ordered washers, pliers and an adjustable spanner. He leant over the sink and began fiddling with the tap while Grandma looked on, bursting with maternal pride. My mother meanwhile was busy laying out the birthday supper on the dining table. I looked out the window, to see my aunt and her family drive up in their Holden Commodore Executive.

After the greetings were exchanged, we all sat around the table with Grandma at the head, to watch her slowly open each present as it was given. After she had carefully folded the last piece of wrapping paper, she turned towards my mother.

'I don't like to mention these things, Ivy,' my grandmother said. 'But haven't you put on a little weight?' She paused, before calling for backup from my aunt. 'What do you think, Priscilla?'

'I think you may be right,' she agreed, stuffing a second piece of cake into her own slim little mouth.

'I've been going swimming twice a week lately, but it doesn't seem to be helping.'

'Swimming! What a sight that must be.'

'When she gets out of the water,' my father sniggered, 'she could be mistaken for a beached whale.'

That's the kind of guy good old Dad is.

'At least she's trying,' I said, 'which is more than can be said for you, with your big fat gut.'

Everybody turned to face me. My father made a slapping gesture in my direction, a joke-kind of a slap, except that it wasn't.

'Perhaps I should visit a gym a couple of times a week as well,' sighed my mother. They spun back to focus on her again.

'Oh, but gym memberships are so expensive, aren't they?' Grandma frowned.

Meaning that my mother wastes far too much of my father's hard-earned money already.

'Nice cake, Mum,' I said and would have smiled at her except that she was looking miserably down at her plate.

'Now tell me, Sharon, how's school going?' asked my grandmother.

Sharon, my cousin who is a year younger than me, then detailed her latest exam results (all excellent, of course) and the grade she was now in with her violin (the highest), until I was almost vomiting on the carpet. Her brother, Craig, then spoke about the sporting trophies he'd just won, as well as a scuba course he was doing.

'By the way,' I suddenly found myself blurting out, 'I have an apprenticeship with a garage.'

Everyone looked at me immediately.

'You're not still wanting to be a motor mechanic, are you?' sniffed my grandmother.

'Yep. And now I've got an actual apprenticeship. I started a while ago.'

'An apprenticeship! My goodness! Isn't there any other job you could get?' Grandma looked disapprovingly at my mother, who just shrugged her shoulders and began clearing the table.

'Well, mechanics certainly know how to charge like wounded bulls,' said my uncle. 'I took my car in for a service the other day, just a straight-forward service, and I almost had to take out a bank loan to pay for it.'

My father had his own story to tell about a rip-off mechanic and the two men got up from the table, deep in conversation. Sharon went into the kitchen to help my mother do the dishes, while Grandma and Priscilla moved to more comfortable lounge chairs. Craig smiled awkwardly at me, before leaping to his feet and rushing away. I was left alone at the table. All of a sudden, a parcel was placed in front of me.

'What's this?'

'Happy birthday,' Priscilla said.

'Oh, thanks.'

I opened the package. Inside was a bright yellow T-shirt.

'Wow,' I said. 'This will certainly stop me from getting run over when I cross the road.'

'What a lovely cheerful colour,' said my grandmother, appearing at my elbow.

'I explained to the salesgirl that my adopted niece was having a special birthday, and she suggested this,' Priscilla added.

Adopted niece? Why on earth did she bother to mention that? And why did Priscilla think that the salesgirl would have any interest in whether the customer's niece was a blood relative or a ring-in? I could feel all the blood, all the adopted blood, rushing to my face.

'Why did the salesgirl suggest yellow? Are nieces colour-coded these days? What's the colour for real nieces? Red? Sorry, but I don't want this t-shirt.'

My grandmother slammed her fist down on the table and shouted, 'You ungrateful girl! Priscilla didn't have to buy you anything. Once again, you've proved to us all that you don't deserve to be part of this family.'

Out of the corner of my eye, I could see Sharon smirking, tea towel suspended mid-air.

'I'm a Walsh. That's my name. Same as you.'

'No, you may pretend to be a Walsh,' screamed my grandmother, furiously stabbing at me through the air with her finger, 'but we all know that you're not. You weren't born a Walsh and the truth is that you'll NEVER be one!'

'Take your precious goddamn family and stick them all up your arse!'

I flung the T-shirt against the wall and stormed out, slamming the door as hard as I could behind me.

I waited in the carport for my parents to come out of the house. When they finally did appear, an hour and a half later, they didn't say a word to me and so in total silence, we drove home through the pouring rain. I knew that my father felt disgraced and humiliated by me – he'd told me often enough for me to get the picture. My mother sobbed quietly into a handkerchief, going down her well-worn path of self-blame for my bad behaviour, her weight, and of course her infertility – even though it was my father's low sperm count that had been the problem.

From the back seat, I watched the wet bitumen road flash beneath the car. Grandma was right; I wasn't a Walsh and believe me, I was grateful for that. But I didn't know my real name, or where my real family was. I looked at the gutters filling up with water, blocked by all the unwanted, useless crap that people had thrown away earlier. Garbage just like me.

If Jess hadn't dragged me out of bed the next day, I doubt that I would've bothered to sit for my licence. I got through the written test okay, but almost lost it when I realised that Jess wasn't allowed in the car with me for the driving part. She took me aside and eyeballed me, before handing me back to the examiner. I drove the route I was instructed to follow, did an acceptable three-point turn and parallel park, and remembered to count to three at the stop sign before I moved off. I got my licence. Jess was thrilled, but I was past caring. I insisted on sitting in the passenger's seat on the way home, and the minute I could, crawled back into bed and pulled the covers up over my head. There I stayed until the next morning, when I had to get up to go to work. At least in the garage I wasn't a complete waste of space.

FOUND
(Jess)

Poor Nikki. She'd clearly had a shocking eighteenth birthday and I felt quite sorry for her. Why do families always have to behave so appallingly? Her story reminded me of my own birthday debacle earlier in the year. Because it had been my twenty-first, my parents had insisted on throwing a huge party, inviting the entire neighbourhood even though I'd made it perfectly plain that I had wanted something small. My father drank too much and stumbled his way through a humiliating, sentimental speech about 'his little girl'. Even worse, was my mother's behaviour. She spent most of the party giggling out on the terrace, ensconced in some old hippy's lap, as the two of them shared a batch of dope cookies. I wish that I could expunge that mental image of my mother entirely from my memory, and indeed the whole dreadful night.

However, stressing about my own dysfunctional family didn't shed any light on Nikki's and besides, I soon realised that the fallout from her birthday wasn't yet over.

'I've decided,' Nikki announced at The Purple Crush a week later, 'that I'm going to find my mother.'

'Who?'

'My birth mother.'

'Isn't one enough of a hassle?'

'But she's my real mother. It'll be different with her.'

'How can you say that? You haven't even met her.'

Nikki glared at me. 'You don't understand. She gave birth to me.'

I wondered if it was actually that simple. Someone who conceives, carries a foetus for nine months, gives birth and then abandons the baby – is that what constitutes motherhood? Personally, I didn't think so.

'But you haven't seen her for eighteen years,' I said aloud. 'She's never made contact or even bothered about your birthday during all of this time. How can there be any sort of bond between you?'

'Of course there will be,' Nikki snapped. 'I have her genes, I'm her biological child. You don't get a closer connection than that.'

'Right,' I said, dubiously.

'After all, "blood is thicker than water", as they say.'

'Yes, "blood *is* thicker than water . . . but then so is soup!" That's another wise old saying.'

'No, that's just stupid!'

Nikki picked up a cue and sent a ball ricocheting around the table. It was a miracle that it didn't become airborne.

'Anyway,' she continued, 'I may even have a sister.'

I resisted the temptation to offer her mine.

'Or a brother.'

I remained silent.

'A whole family. I wonder if they spend Christmas together. Perhaps they all go away to some beach house for the week.'

Why did Nikki imagine that her perfect family existed, just waiting to be found? This was sheer fantasy-land. And her concept of a week-long happy family gathering at Christmas-time? Utterly delusional!

'Have you told your parents that you're looking for your mother?'

'No way.'

'Shouldn't you at least let them know?'

Nikki emphatically shook her head.

'Jess,' she suddenly said, 'I have to do this. I need to find out who I am, and where I belong.'

Not knowing how to respond without putting my foot in it, I simply smiled an acknowledgment, took the pool cue from her and had my shot. I sank four balls in a row. At least the fact that I was winning the game served to distract her for the moment.

Fortunately for Nikki, now that she had her driving licence, she was no longer trapped at home and instead could spend all of her free time in her beloved car. She leapt at any opportunity to attach her two feet to those pedals, and so drove Amanda to the bank, Daniel to buy parts for his car and Aunty Lil to the supermarket. As for me, Nikki helped me move.

It had taken me longer than I had hoped to find a flat, as most were out of my price range. I'd also had another impediment at the start – the local real estate agent who was in charge of rental properties.

'Do you have a boyfriend?' he asked, winking sleazily at me.

'And what relevance does that have?'

'Just asking. Can you afford a little more rent?'

'No, I've told you what I can pay. That's it, no more.'

'Does your boyfriend stay over a lot? Perhaps he could pitch in some extra money?'

The slimy turd! As if I was the sort of woman who needed to be 'financially looked after' by a boyfriend. However, I certainly wasn't about to let him know that there was no boyfriend, cashed-up or otherwise.

After this exchange, I stopped returning his phone calls and eventually managed to find a flat that was advertised by a different real estate agency in the local paper. It wasn't a particularly attractive flat, but I could afford the rent and the bond, so I'd signed up. Nikki offered to borrow someone's trailer and so, the next Saturday morning, she arrived at my sister's flat.

'Where is she?' she asked, peering through doorways.

'Who?'

Nikki raised her eyebrows at me.

'She's not here. Gone away for the weekend,' I lied. In fact, I'd only managed to get my sister out of the place for the day.

We loaded the few possessions I had at the flat into the trailer and were discussing the best way to get to the storage warehouse, when it began to rain. We rapidly relocated everything onto the back seat of The Beast, then jumped into my car to go to the hardware store to buy a tarp.

'Hey, what's this?' Nikki asked, picking up a jacket from the floor.

I glanced across. 'That belongs to Max.'

'Max? Who's Max?'

'Just a guy I met at that rally.'

'I was there too, but I don't remember a Max.'

'I met him after you and the others had left.'

'We didn't leave, we went to get some drinks. So who is he?'

'I've already said, just a guy.'

'Meaning?'

'You want a dossier on him?'

Nikki ignored my tone. 'Especially if there's a photo in it.'

Thankfully we arrived at the shop. However, the instant we were back in the car, she grabbed the jacket again and began re-examining it.

'My guess is that he's short, wears glasses and has a concave chest. Am I right?'

'Sure,' I scoffed. Did she truly think that I was going to fall for that old fishing routine, when I'd been the one to teach it to her?

'Aha!' Nikki exclaimed suddenly. 'He has long hair, light brown, or is it red?'

Fortunately I was stopped at a traffic light. 'Let me see that.'

Nikki passed over the strand of hair that she was studying.

'Yes, that belongs to Max.' I gave it back to her. The lights turned green.

'Not just a guy, I think, Jess. If he was, you would've dropped that hair on the floor.'

Bloody hell! Why was Nikki sometimes so perceptive? I sighed and gave in.

'Actually, Max has chestnut hair. He's extremely smart and very politically astute. Plus he's got a great sense of humour.'

'What does he drive?'

'He rides a push bike.'

Nikki recovered quickly from her disappointment, to continue prodding.

'And?'

'He's a student, doing Politics and Economics.'

'Yes?'

I hesitated.

'So?' she insisted.

'So nothing,' I stated firmly. 'I'm not interested in having a boyfriend right now. Okay, so maybe I do like him a little bit, but I'm actually happy just being friends.'

Back outside my sister's flat, I pulled in behind The Beast with its trailer.

'Look, it's stopped raining!' Nikki said, stepping out of my car. 'We didn't need to buy the tarp, after all.'

Nevertheless, it did come in handy to line the bottom of the trailer when we reached the storage warehouse, so that my many boxes of books would stay dry underneath. Nikki tried to veto my concrete blocks, and I had to explain that they were a crucial part of the whole bookcase system before she allowed them to be loaded.

By 4:20 pm I had officially moved into my new flat and was surrounded by all of my possessions. Surveying the chaos of boxes and garbage bags, I smoked a cigarette, flicking the ash into the sink, while Nikki wandered aimlessly around. I couldn't even offer her a cup of coffee, because even if by some miracle, I could manage to locate the cups, the kettle, the coffee, the sugar and perhaps even a spoon – I didn't have any milk. And there was little point in buying any, as I didn't have a fridge. I decided that shopping for a fridge was Priority #1.

I asked Nikki to help me assemble the bedframe, before realising that I had no hammer. However this didn't deter my friend, who cleverly transformed her car wheel brace into a makeshift hammer and it looked great when it was all set up. Then I turned my attention to the trendy clothes rack on wheels, which I had borrowed from a friend of my sister's. Not knowing how to hang jeans on it, I ended up simply slinging them over the top bar. Satisfied with my progress,

I walked back into the living room to be confronted by an absolute disaster zone. I looked at Nikki and she at me.

'Feel like shooting a few balls?' I asked.

She nodded.

It was a relief to close the door.

Four hours later, after several games of pool plus dinner, I returned to my new home alone. A cursory search failed to uncover any bed linen, but did deliver up my old sleeping bag. Tomorrow, I thought as I drifted off to sleep, I would buy some long-life milk so that at least I could have a coffee.

However, I didn't have to drink that terrible stuff for long. Amanda found me a free fridge, and even organised Daniel to help deliver it. Max donated a kitchen table and some chairs, justifying his kindness by saying that as a frequent visitor, he was merely looking after his own interests. Sometimes he brought over a bottle of wine, which added fuel to our already-heated political debates, but then one day he turned up with a bunch of flowers. 'For the table,' he explained quickly, after noticing the expression on my face. I knew that he wouldn't make the same mistake again and I was glad that I'd nipped that one in the old proverbial bud.

One night, only ten minutes after Max had left, I was brushing my teeth when the phone rang. I looked at my watch, walked into the sitting room and picked up the phone.

'What,' I said, rather crossly. 'It's midnight.'

'It's me.'

I wiped the toothpaste from my mouth with the back of my hand. 'This had better be important, Nikki. I'm trying to go to bed, not a particularly outrageous thing to do at this time of night, I believe.'

There was no response.

'Nikki?'

'I know it's late but . . .' Her voice trailed off.

'Are you alright?'

'I guess so.'

'Well then, can you ring back in the morning?'

'Okay.'

I was just about to hang up when I heard a soft, squelchy sniff. Nikki was crying? She never cries.

'Wait. What's up?'

'I . . . This afternoon I went . . . It was . . .'

'You rang me in the middle of the night in order to stutter incoherently into the phone?' I said, but my attempt at humour was met with silence. I was grateful for the long telephone cord so that I could sit down on the couch. This was clearly going to take some time.

'Nikki, what's happened?'

'I've . . . I've found out who my mother is,' she whispered.

'Wow. But isn't that good news? So Jigsaw finally got back in touch with you?'

'No. I mean yes. That was last week. They called and told me that they weren't able to make contact with my mother.'

'What? Didn't you just say that you know who she is? Sorry, I'm confused.'

I heard Nikki exhale loudly.

'Actually, I found out by accident, because Births, Deaths and Marriages Registry made a mistake. I needed a full birth certificate to apply for a passport, but when I picked it up, there were two certificates inside the envelope – one for me as an adopted kid and the other was my real one, which they weren't meant to give me.'

'So the original birth certificate had your parents' names on it?'

'Just my mother's.'

'Are you going to get in touch with her?'

'Too right I am.'

'Then this is great, isn't it?'

'No. I didn't realise who it was going to turn out to be.'

'What? You already know her?'

'Know her?' Nikki suddenly shouted. 'Yes, I know her! Or at least I goddamn thought that I knew her!'

'I don't understand.'

'She's Aunty Lil!'

'What?'

'Aunty Lil is my mother.' Her voice was bitter.

'Oh! Are you sure?'

'That's what it says on the birth certificate.'

'This is a hell of a shock.'

'Tell me about it.'

'I guess that it could've been a whole lot worse, couldn't it?' I said. 'After all, you've always got on well with Lil and . . .'

But Nikki screamed down the phone, 'Don't you understand anything? My entire life has been based on a goddamn LIE!'

I heard a loud bang, like something metal being kicked.

'What was that?' I asked.

'Nothing.'

'Where are you?'

'In a phone box.'

'Where?'

'Morris Street.'

'What are you doing over there?'

'Where do you suggest I should be? At home with my family of lying arseholes?'

I heard another thump.

'Do you want to stay here for the night? Jump in your car and come over.'

'I can't.'

'Why not?'

'No car.'

Where on earth was The Beast?

'I'll come and get you. Morris Street is off Ferang, right? See you soon.'

I put down the phone, threw on a jumper, grabbed my car keys and drove to the phone box. Nikki was sitting outside on the pavement, her feet in the gutter.

'Hey, gorgeous! Want a lift?' I called.

But my friend was in no mood for jokes, or talking, so we drove back in silence while Nikki gazed out of the car window. Once we were home again, she collapsed onto the couch.

'Got any bourbon?' she asked.

'No. So . . . your mother is Aunty Lil!'

'I still can't really believe it.'

'It must have been such a shock.'

'I don't get it. Aunty Lil is a Christian. Over the years she's given me five Bibles! Five! She even wears a bloody wedding ring, saying that she's married to God!'

'That's incredibly hypocritical,' I snorted.

'Why didn't they tell me? Why was it kept such a secret?'

'I have no idea.'

'How can I have been so stupid? Do you know what they used to tell me?'

I didn't answer. I was starting to feel out of my depth.

'Mum has always said that my birth mother was a sixteen-year-old girl who couldn't look after a baby. What absolute BULLSHIT! I've worked out that Lil must have been thirty-five when she had me. How can they have lied to me for all these years? They were all in on the secret, including Grandma. The joke is certainly on me.' Nikki's hands were clenched in rage.

'And what about your father?' I asked quietly.

'Of course Dad was part of it. Hilarious.'

'No, I mean your biological father.'

'How should I know? I'm the last person to be told anything!' Nikki shouted. 'On the birth certificate it says that my father is unknown.'

It was all much too much. I thought of my own family and realised that at least I've always known who my parents are, even if I wasn't thrilled about it.

'I never want to see that woman again. I hate her guts! Why didn't she tell me that she was my mother? And then there's Dad. He used to carry on about my bad genes every time I did something he didn't approve of, which naturally was all the time. What an absolute bastard! Grandma too must've known that I was really a Johnstone and not a Walsh. And as for Mum . . .'

'Which Mum?' I asked. It was all quite bewildering.

'My adopted mother . . . my real aunt . . . whichever!' Nikki furiously snatched her wallet out of her back pocket and hurled it against the wall. I stood up to retrieve it but stopped when I heard a strange howling noise. I looked around to see tears streaming down Nikki's face.

'Why didn't she want me?' she wailed. 'Why did she throw me away?'

I went over to sit beside her, but couldn't think of a single comforting thing to say. After all, Lil had made the choice to relinquish her baby, and nothing that I could say was going to change that simple fact. So I just sat beside my friend, rubbing her gently on the back, and eventually she stopped crying.

'Sorry about the waterworks,' Nikki said, wiping her face with her sleeve. I got up and passed her a box of tissues. 'I guess you were wondering if it was ever going to end.'

'Nobody can cry forever.'

'Can't they?' she frowned, her eyes tearing up again.

'Nup! Everyone has to take a break now and then, to dry out the hankies.'

'But isn't that why tissues were invented?' Nikki threw the box of tissues at me and we both sort of smiled.

'So where's The Beast?'

'On the side of the road near the city.'

'What's it doing there?'

Nikki groaned. 'After seeing that birth certificate, I didn't know what to do, so I just drove around. I'm not sure where I even went.'

'You shouldn't have been driving.'

'I know that,' she snapped. 'Which is why eventually I decided to pull over. But there was a Honda Accord on my left, that I hadn't seen.'

'Please tell me you didn't run into it.'

'I spun the wheel sharply, swerving and skidding all over the place, and the driver gave me the finger as he zoomed off.'

'Hurray, you missed it!'

'Yeah, but I slammed into a post.'

'What?'

'An old white post on the side of the road.'

'How much damage did you do?'

'Dunno. I didn't look. I could see that the engine was leaking water underneath so I just grabbed my things and started to walk.'

'Oh Nikki.'

She slumped even further down on the couch, looking exhausted. I went to find her a sleeping bag and a pillow.

'Try to get some sleep,' I said, handing them both over. 'Need anything else?'

She shook her head, so I said goodnight and headed for bed. I'm not sure if she stayed up for much longer because the minute I was between the sheets, I myself fell asleep.

LOST
(Nikki)

Where the bloody hell was my wallet? I was sure that I hadn't left it behind in The Beast yesterday, but it wasn't in any of my pockets or in my bag.

'What's up?' asked Jess, emerging from her bedroom.

'I've lost my wallet.'

'Hmm. I think I know where it is.' She walked over to the far corner of the room, looked around and then retrieved something from underneath a chair. It was my wallet.

'Thanks. How did it get over there?'

'You don't remember? Anyway, aren't you late for work?'

'Nah, I've already called in sick. I can't face the garage today.'

'Fair enough.'

'I thought I might go and see good old Aunty Lil instead.'

'Really?'

'I've got some questions I want to put to her.'

'Good luck!' Jess said, looking at her watch. 'Well, I'd better be off. I've got a Finances Committee meeting in half an hour.' She grabbed an apple and stuffed it into her backpack. 'Are you sure you're okay?'

'I'm fine!'

But she just stood there.

'Bye,' I said, squeezing my lips into a smile.

That did the trick. Jess slung her backpack over one shoulder and left.

I caught a train and a bus, and then, with shaking hands, I knocked on the door of Lil's house.

'Nicola! Why aren't you at work?' she cried as she opened the door.

I stared at her. It was as if I'd never seen this woman before in my life, and yet at the same time, I wanted to punch her.

'I decided to take the day off today,' I said, somehow managing to keep my voice steady as I followed her down the hallway. 'I wanted to come and see you.'

'Oh. Is everything all right?'

'Yes, fine,' I said but I guess that she could tell by my expression that it wasn't.

'How's your mother?' she asked, handing me a can of Coke. 'Was she able to get an appointment at the hospital before Christmas?'

'Which mother?' I snorted.

'I beg your pardon?'

'How should I know? That's her business. Ring her yourself if you're so goddamn interested.'

'Nicola, what's wrong with you today?'

'Nothing.'

'Have a seat. Your pacing is getting on my nerves.'

'No.' I continued to roam around the room, picking things up and putting them down again.

'Aunt Rose bought me that,' she said when I pretended to examine a bottle with coloured, layered sand in it. 'I think she got it when she was on holiday in—'

'I know that you're my mother,' I blurted out.

'Pardon?'

'You're my mother, aren't you?'

Aghast, she just looked at me.

'Answer me!' I yelled.

She remained speechless.

'Your name is on my birth certificate.'

Still nothing.

'Why won't you speak? Lost for words because I finally know who you are?'

'Have you finished your Coke?' she finally said, looking at the floor. 'Would you like another?'

'What? Did you hear what I said?'

'How's your car going?'

'Are you deaf?'

'Can you please stop shouting?'

'Haven't you got anything to say to me?'

'I don't understand why you're being so difficult today.'

'Difficult?'

'Is there a problem at work? Is that why you didn't go?'

I stared at her, completely gobsmacked. The colour had returned to her cheeks. I don't think I've hated anyone as much as I hated her at that moment.

'I've got to go. There's no point in staying.'

I walked towards the front door, with her trailing behind.

'Would you like a sandwich first, dear?'

I turned to face her and looked her straight in the eyes. 'You're my real mother. How did that happen?'

'Don't be absurd, Nicola. I don't want to hear any more of this ridiculous nonsense,' she said firmly. 'You're my favourite niece and that's that.'

'What? You're saying that you're not my mother?'

'I will always be your Aunty Lil.'

I raced out the door, into the street, and just kept on running. Only when I was struggling to catch my breath, did I slow down to a walk. How dare that woman pretend that she wasn't my mother! Why the hell was she lying? Did she really think that I was going to swallow such bullshit when I knew the truth?

Suddenly I looked around and realised that I had no idea where I was. Where was the nearest goddamn train station? I went into a milk bar to ask for directions, but the guy behind the counter wasn't a local and just shrugged his shoulders. I kept wandering, until finally I stumbled across a sign with an arrow and managed to find my way to some train station in the middle of nowhere.

I found an empty part of a platform and parked myself on a bench seat. I sat there for hours, watching trains pull in and out and people get on and off. Mid-afternoon, a large group of secondary school boys crowded onto the platform, jostling and shouting at each other. I began to think that it was time to move on, and when I saw somebody dressed as Father Christmas sitting in a carriage, I decided to join him and so jumped on board. I must've fallen asleep because I was jolted awake by somebody yelling. I opened my eyes to discover a railway attendant, standing there in an empty carriage, ordering me off the train. I left the station and began to wander aimlessly around the streets.

Dusk fell and lights were switched on inside houses. I took refuge in a bus shelter. A young couple walked past, holding a small child by the hand and pushing a pram. One perfect happy little family. I kicked the side of the shelter, hard, and the mother turned to stare.

'What the fuck are you gawking at!' I yelled.

She said something to her husband, who quickly picked up the child, and together they scurried away into the night.

It started to drizzle. I stood up and felt the fine drops of rain fall on my face. It was almost soothing. Suddenly a small shape caught my eye as it moved towards me.

'Hey little doggie,' I said to the scruffy dog sniffing around the bus shelter. I patted her and she leapt up onto the bench to sit beside me. Her coat was quite damp and she seemed hungry. A search of my pockets revealed a left-over corner of a biscuit, which she gobbled up as if she hadn't eaten for weeks. I checked my other pockets while she waited patiently, but only found crumbs.

'Are you lost? No home to go to?' I stroked her fur gently and she pricked up her ears, listening. 'Don't worry,' I told her, 'I'll look after you.'

But all of a sudden, she twirled around and jumped off the seat. 'Don't leave. Please stay,' I begged, but she'd already gone. It was then that I heard what the dog had caught on the wind.

'Monty! Where are you?' Way down the street someone was calling. I could just make out a figure bending down to greet a wriggling small shadow.

I burst into tears, bawling like a baby. I don't think that I've ever felt so alone in my entire life. I didn't even care if anybody saw or heard me.

Eventually I managed to pull myself together and stood up. Catching a couple of trains and buses, I made it home and was grateful that my parents were already in bed. I hugged Panadol for a while, grabbed a few clothes and rang the garage's answering machine to say that I had the flu. Finally I scribbled a note explaining that I was going away for a while, which I left on my pillow, and rushed back into the night. At Spencer Street Station, I bought a ticket for the next departing regional train and within the hour, I had left Melbourne and was heading for somewhere else.

I don't actually remember much of my time away. I hit the Jim Beam and Coke pretty hard, alternating between drinking and sleeping, so the days passed in a fog, and way too quickly. I thought of staying there for good, but realised that I'd soon run out of money. Bourbon wasn't cheap. So back I had to come, ready or not.

It was Sunday evening when I arrived home. I marched straight into the living room and switched off the TV, which immediately got the attention of my parents. I took a deep breath.

'I know the truth,' I announced.

'Hey! We're watching a show!' My father began searching for the remote control.

'Where have you been?' asked my mother.

'I know what you've been hiding all these years.'

'What are you talking about?'

'No more dirty little secret!'

'Nikki, I really don't understand what you're saying.'

I eyeballed my mother but to my surprise, she seemed to be genuinely bewildered. However I saw that my father's face had turned a deep shade of red.

'John,' said my mother, noticing too, 'do you know what Nikki is talking about?'

My father leapt to his feet and switched the TV back on. I stood there, completely dumbfounded by their behaviour, as they became engrossed in their show again. Moments passed.

'By the way, Nikki,' my mother said. 'I talked to Lil the other day. She's furious with you. Did you two have a fight?'

'What have you done now?' groaned my father.

'What have I done?' I echoed, incredulous.

I stormed out of the living room and escaped into my bedroom. I flung myself face down on the bed. What the hell just happened? Could my mother really not know the truth? Yet why was my father looking so goddamn guilty? Did he know, but my mother didn't? No, that didn't make sense. Could I be Lil's dirty little secret, that not even her sisters were aware of? I took out my birth certificate and inspected it for the millionth time. In black and white, for all to see, there was the name Lily Johnstone in the column for my mother. I hadn't made it up. But it was starting to dawn on me that perhaps nobody knew the truth about my birth, except for Lil, of course . . . and now me.

On Tuesday after work, I went to TAFE to meet up with Jess for our usual game of pool, glad to be doing something normal for a change. The toilets were packed, which meant that I had to wait for Jess in the far corner, out of everyone's way.

'At last!' I shouted when she eventually appeared.

'Why didn't you return my calls?' she yelled back.

Someone started up the hand drier for the hundredth time.

'What?'

'Where have you been?'

'Away. Come on, let's go!'

But Jess still didn't make a move.

'Where were you?'

'Nowhere in particular. Okay, I ended up in Bairnsdale, if you must know.'

'Where did you stay?'

'In some kind of youth hostel. What's with all the questions?'

'When did you get back?'

'Sunday.'

Jess disappeared into a cubicle. I watched clouds of smoke drift over the top of the door, and I overheard a couple of girls complaining. Fair enough, I thought. It's a disgusting habit. I leant up against the wall while one by one, everybody left. Finally, there was peace.

'Nikki,' Jess shouted, bursting out of the cubicle, 'you're an unbelievable little turd.'

Clearly I'd done something wrong, again. 'Take a number and join the queue,' I said. 'But I'm warning you, there's a lot of people ahead of you waiting to abuse me.'

'Why didn't you phone me? Even if it was just once?'

'What?' Didn't Jess understand that I was already trying to deal with a whole heap of crap and didn't need her to pile on any more?

'I don't know why I waste my time on you!'

'Neither do I,' I agreed and sighed.

'Oh.' There was a pause before she added, 'I shouldn't have said that. So you went away?'

'Yeah, I couldn't hang around. It didn't work out with Lil, you know.'

'Actually, I don't. You never got around to telling me.'

'Do you want to know, or not?'

'Yes. So what happened?'

'In a word – nothing. When I said that I knew that she was my mother, she pretended not to have heard. She kept repeating that I was her niece.'

'She denied it?'

'Not exactly. More like she refused to acknowledge me as her daughter.'

'But you have the proof.'

'Yes, but she made it abundantly clear that she doesn't want to claim me as hers. She didn't want me when I was born, and she still doesn't. She must be really ashamed of me and honestly, I don't blame her. I am a total loser.' I scowled at my reflection in the mirror.

'What are you saying? That it's all your fault?' Jess spun me around to face her and gave me a little shake. 'No, Nikki, it's got nothing to do with you. Just think about it for a minute. There's Lil, who—'

'Think about it? I've been doing nothing else!'

'Listen, Lil has been hiding this secret for years, so of course she's going to have a major problem readjusting. Besides,' Jess said as she swivelled me back towards the mirror, 'who's the one Lil calls her favourite niece?'

Our eyes met in the mirror.

'Jess, I'm her only niece.'

'I know, but the fact still remains that you've always been special to her.'

'It felt like being rejected by my mother all over again.'

'For sure. But obviously it was simply too much for her and she couldn't adjust. It's going to take her some time to come around.'

Jess had no idea how stubborn Lil can be, but I let it pass.

'Somehow I thought that when I found my real mother, everything would be different. I'd be different, and that my life would change. But it isn't better. In fact, it's a whole heap worse because I've discovered that it's all based on a lie.'

'Did you ask Lil about your father?'

'You've got to be joking. She denied being my mother – she certainly wasn't going to talk about the father of the daughter she doesn't have!'

'So you got nowhere? Found out zilch?'

'Put it this way, a budgie could've given away more information than Lil.'

'And what about your other mother? How's she handling it?' Jess asked.

'That's even weirder.'

'What?'

'I don't think they know.'

'Seriously?'

'Yes.'

'How can that be?'

'Not a clue.'

'Now this doesn't make any sense at all.'

'I agree.'

We looked at each other in silence for a minute.

'What a mess.'

'Absolutely.'

'Why didn't you ring me, Nikki?'

'I wasn't near a phone.'

'You should have found one. I was worried about you.'

'How come?'

'Because I'm your friend, stupid.'

'Oh.' Clearly she was waiting for more, so I added, 'Thanks?'

'Bloody hell, Nikki! Anyway, I'm glad you're back.'

'Good. Can we play pool now?'

She nodded and so finally, a bloody hour late, we made it to The Purple Crush.

Likewise Fred tried to be nice to me, but was also very annoying. He helped me tow The Beast back to the garage and gave me some money towards the parking fines that had been stuck on the windscreen. A Christmas bonus, he said, and began whistling along to a Christmas carol that was playing on the radio. It was okay for him. He had a happy, normal family – just like Jess and the whole rest of the goddamn world. At work I wore my safety ear muffs all the time, to protect myself from those disgusting carols. Christmas was absolute crap, and for complete suckers. I wanted nothing to do with it.

CROSSING INTO ENEMY TERRITORY
(Jess)

I remembered the instant I woke up that it was Christmas Day, but it took me a little longer to realise where I was. It had been a long time since I'd stayed the night in my mother's house at The Bend. I sat up in bed to examine my old bedroom. Everything was much the same as it always was, with posters still gracing the walls of Eddy Charlton and Nelson Mandela, two great heroes of mine when I was a teenager – both men, I now noted.

I got up and found my mother Kate in the kitchen, barely covered by a sarong. She kissed me and raised a coffee pot towards me as a question. I nodded, and she gestured towards the door.

I walked outside to take a seat at the immense wooden table that was in the shady part of the garden. I lit a cigarette, inhaling deeply.

'Darling, I really wish you wouldn't smoke,' my mother said as she approached, carrying a tray laden with pottery dishes. 'It's bad for your health, and the environment. Including my own little piece of the environment.'

As if the air surrounding her twenty-five hectares of bush was going to be contaminated by my cigarette smoke.

'Well, I wish that you wouldn't walk around the house half-naked,' I countered, pouring my coffee.

Kate ran her fingers through her long hair, as she always does when she's annoyed, and took a sip of her peppermint tea. We sat there in silence for a while, watching the birds taking turns at the water dish. I was the first to surrender.

'It's beautiful here,' I said. 'I'd forgotten.'

'It's been a while since you've visited.'

I ignored her reproach. 'When's Krishna coming over?'

'Around 11. And be warned, she's bringing presents.'

'What?'

'I'm just telling you so that you're prepared.'

'But it's so ridiculously capitalist and consumerist. Why does she want to be part of that crap?'

'It's important to your sister and therefore we have to receive her gifts in the spirit in which they are given.' She delivered her hippy philosophy with a smile, but I was well aware of the edict lurking beneath.

I finished my coffee and lit another cigarette, just as a slight breeze made the wind chimes sound. We heard footsteps from around the side of the house and there was Dad. I leapt up to give him a kiss. He went into the kitchen, got himself a mug and presented it to my mother for coffee. 'Happy Christmas to my two beautiful girls,' he said, before removing his sandals and settling more comfortably into his chair. He then added, 'So when's lunch?'

Kate and I exchanged a look. My father knew perfectly well that my mother wasn't responsible for the timing of lunch, but every year he never failed to ask that question. In reply, she went inside and reappeared with a ceramic plate laden with beautiful tropical fruit, which she placed in front of him. Her fruit platters are considered to be the best in The Bend, and Dad grinned happily as the juice trickled down his beard with each mouthful.

I decided to have a shower and get dressed. When I returned, my parents were deep in conversation about some new Council environmental strategy. They're both one-eyed greenies, but neither actually dirty their hands with being politically active.

Eventually Dad turned to me.

'So tell me, my darling, how's things with you?' he asked.

'Terrific. I've been—' I began, only to be interrupted by the appearance of Jane, my father's partner and Dylan, their ten-year-old son. I hugged them both, before Dylan disappeared into the house to get himself his usual glass of homemade lemon cordial. He had grown a lot since I'd last seen him. He was clearly going to be tall, like Dad.

'I think the coffee's cold now. I'll make a fresh pot,' said my mother.

'I'll make some tea as well,' Jane proposed. 'Henry and Mira weren't far behind us on the path.' Henry, Jane's brother, and Mira, his partner, only ever drink tea.

'How's your course going?' my father asked, turning his attention back to me again. 'I'd really like to know.'

'It's okay and my job at the Student Union is—' I broke off to welcome Henry and Mira plus their three kids, who were followed in quick succession by Liz, Mum's nearest neighbour, and her two teenage sons, both carrying chairs under their arms.

The kissing, hugging and cries of 'Happy Christmas' were barely over, when my sister arrived.

'Merry Merries!' Krishna bellowed over the noise of the crowd, brandishing several bottles of champagne. She was wearing one of those absurd red felt Santa hats. She did the rounds of greeting each person in turn, as if she were the star attraction everyone had come to see, with her boyfriend trailing behind in her wake. Mum's neighbours from the adjoining valley, all six of them, then showed up and I decided that it was time to make some phone calls.

At the kitchen door, I turned and looked back at the large gathering in the garden. The children were sprawled across the ground, intent on making costumes and hats to wear at lunch. Mira seemed to be the one in charge of the scissors. The teenagers were either ensconced in hammocks, or clustered together in small groups. My mother was showing Krishna around the garden, their heads almost touching as they examined individual plants. At the table, everyone was laughing uproariously at the joke that my father had just told. It must have been very funny. Suddenly Jane became aware that I was standing there, alone, and beckoned me over to where she sat. I shook my head, waved and escaped indoors.

I rang Nikki first. She wasn't home and her parents had no idea where she was. They sounded quite angry. Poor Nikki was clearly not coping and I wondered where on earth she'd gone, this time. I wished that I'd thought ahead, and had given her the key to my flat.

Next up, I called Max and was lucky to catch him as he was just about to head to his parents' place for lunch. He asked about my Christmas, to which I replied vaguely that it was a quiet family affair with just my parents and my sister, grateful for the muting effect of mud brick walls.

I hung up as quickly as I could, because I knew that I didn't have long. Sure enough, just as I'd put down the phone, my father came into the sitting room. Preparations for the Christmas Feast were about to begin, and I was being summoned.

Every year, for the past eight years, the Christmas Feast has taken place in The Barn. I'm not sure why it was originally named this, given that it's not used to house animals, aside from the occasional kangaroo, wallaby or wombat which may take temporary shelter. In actual fact, it was built out of second-hand materials to accommodate local social gatherings of humans. Because there aren't any walls, it's only a suitable venue for parties during summer. The tin roof protects the revellers from rain, unless it's slanting in from the west.

This year there wasn't a cloud in the sky as Dad, Dylan and I walked through the bush to a neighbour's place. Mick was already waiting for us. The four of us immediately loaded six massive trestle tables into the back of his ute, drove a short distance and then hauled them all the way into The Barn – no easy feat. For while The Barn is situated conveniently near a junction of several dirt roads, it's a hundred metres into the bush, which safeguards its seclusion but also makes things extraordinarily difficult for party organisers.

Liz's teenagers turned up with the tablecloths (sheets from the local op shop) and Henry with some chairs borrowed from his workplace. The general rule is that everyone looks after their own seating requirements, but as there are a couple of people in the community whose cars are too small to carry chairs, some extras have to be supplied. Then it was home to assist in Operation Packing. Across the neighbourhood, every household had swung into a similar mode, making final adjustments to dishes of food and emptying contents of refrigerators into eskies. Everything was loaded into cars, unloaded, and then carted with stupendous effort through the bush and into The Barn.

Eventually all the preparations for the Christmas Feast had been done. The assembled multitude slumped into chairs, exhausted, and surveyed the vast array of dishes adorning the tables. The children continued to shout and laugh, dressed in the party hats and costumes which they'd made that morning. Suddenly, someone opened a bottle of champagne and as if a bell had sounded, there was a frenzied grab from all sides for the serving implements. Plates from at least ten different dinner sets were piled high, and assorted cutlery employed into immediate action. There was a symphony of sounds with the opening and closing of esky lids, together with the tinkling of liquids as beverages of all kinds were poured into glasses. Even the children fell silent and the sound of eating filled The Barn, interrupted only by admiring comments about the food.

'So which dish are you responsible for?' Helen, Mick's partner, asked me.

'You've got to be joking,' cut in Krishna quickly. 'There's no way Mum would let either of us into her kitchen. That's her exclusive domain, the source of all her power.'

I stared at my sister. When had she become so perceptive?

'There's nothing stopping you girls from cooking something in your own kitchens and bringing it along,' said my father.

Krishna and I snorted in unison. 'So which dish are *you* responsible for, Dad?' I asked, knowing full well that our father never cooks. A male hippy can be just as sexist as the next man.

Liz who was seated nearby laughed, but Jane rushed to smooth things over.

'Our Dylan is on his way to becoming a great little chef,' she said. 'His pastry is superlative.'

Why are men considered to be chefs and women cooks? I wondered. And why is it always the mother's role to teach children how to cook, and to shape their sons into better men than their husbands?

'Krishna doesn't need to cook. She goes to cafes,' announced my sister's boyfriend, to everybody's surprise. They were the first words he'd uttered since arriving at The Bend.

'Aren't parties wonderful?' beamed my mother as she floated past. I suspected that she was already pissed or stoned, or both.

'Which reminds me,' said Krishna, grabbing me by the hand and leading me out of The Barn. I groaned loudly when I realised that she was carrying a parcel, wrapped in gaudy Christmas paper, but that didn't deter my sister in the slightest. She enveloped me in a massive hug and enthusiastically passed over the present.

'I hope you like it, Karma,' she said.

I froze. She instantly realised the terrible mistake she'd made, and began to wail.

'I'm sorry, I truly am. Please forgive me, Jess,' she begged. 'I promise that won't happen ever again.'

'Better not,' I muttered, knowing full well that it would.

I unwrapped my present to find 'The Joy Luck Club', a book that I'd been wanting to read all year.

'Wow, Krishna. An excellent choice,' I said, astonished.

'I'm glad you like it.'

'Actually, I really do. Thanks.'

We stood awkwardly there for another minute, before rushing back into The Barn and the safety of a crowd.

Eventually, and not a minute too soon as far as I was concerned, the Christmas Feast was declared over for another year. By this stage, my facial muscles were beginning to ache and I knew that I couldn't keep the smile up for much longer. I spent the next hour helping with the pack-up and saying farewell to everyone, before escaping at last, with my present, a quiche and some vegetables out of my mother's garden.

Once home, I gratefully collapsed into bed and began to read 'The Joy Luck Club', only getting up for food and toilet breaks.

When I finished it, I had a shower and started a new book. I didn't hear from Nikki, and I confess that I didn't try her again. As is my custom, I saw in the New Year from under my doona. On January 2nd at 10:15 am I finished my fourth book and to commemorate the rebirth of normality, washed my hair. The Silly Season had passed and once again, I had miraculously survived. I began to return to all the things that I'd run out of time to do before the madness had struck. By January 4th I was back in full stride. However, little did I realise that I was walking straight into another minefield.

'What did you say, Jess? I couldn't hear you over the noise of the kettle,' shouted Max from the kitchen.

'Do you have a calculator?' I repeated.

'No, but there's one on the computer.'

'Where?'

Max appeared with a cup of coffee, handed it to me, and brought the calculator up on the screen.

I took a sip. 'Did you forget the sugar again?'

'Sorry, your majesty.' Max took the cup away.

I started adding up the Student Union's monthly expenditure. Up until now, I had been providing hand-written reports, so it was good of Max to let me use his computer. A second cup of coffee arrived at my elbow – much better. I drank it as I worked.

'You bastard!' I said to the computer, as the whole document veered to the right of the page. I tried to shift the page margins again, but it just made it worse. I pressed the keys firmly to put them back in their original position. Nothing happened. I ever so carefully moved the markers once more. Half of the page disappeared from view. 'Bugger!'

'A problem?' Max asked from the other side of the thin wall. I heard the sound of a newspaper being folded.

'This computer's not working!'

'What's wrong?' Max came over.

'I just want to move this bit. It's not as if it's anything complicated.'

'This column?'

'No!' I screamed as the wrong part was highlighted. 'Here!' I blocked it myself.

'Okay, now . . .'

'I do this and then . . . See what I mean?'

'Yes, but that's because . . .' He studied my face before continuing on. 'Do you want me to try to help?'

I managed to nod convincingly. He bent down low to examine the screen.

'Hmm. I think I can see what's happened.'

We were so close that his chestnut hair was almost touching my face.

'Sorry,' he said with a smile and flipped his hair over to the other side.

How did he know that I was conscious of his hair? But his attention was back on the computer.

'If we . . . yes . . . this should work.' He leant across me to move the mouse.

I watched his broad hand alternating between the mouse and the keyboard, aware that he was mere centimetres away from me. I had the ridiculous urge to lean my cheek against his shoulder.

'There you are. All fixed,' Max was saying and straightened up.

I was engulfed by a strange sense of loss as he moved away. Speechless, I gazed at him.

Max hesitated. 'That is what you wanted, isn't it?'

I blinked and managed to refocus. 'Yes, that's terrific. Thanks.'

He left the room and after a quick shake of my head, I returned to my report.

'Jess, I think we should talk,' Max called from the kitchen.

'How come?'

'I have something I want to say.'

'Does it have to be right now?'

'Yes.'

I sighed, sat back, lit a cigarette and spun around, but Max didn't appear.

'What's up?' I asked but received no reply. I decided to get in first. 'Okay, I'm sorry,' I said. 'I know I was dreadful over the coffee. I didn't mean to treat you like a slave. When I'm concentrating hard, I guess that I can come across as a bit obnoxious.'

'A bit?' said Max, materialising in the doorway. 'Anyway, that's not what I want to talk to you about.'

'Oh. So can I rescind my admission of guilt?'

'Very funny. Anyway, my question to you is this: Why are guys still expected to make the first move?'

'I've stopped work for this? Can't we have this discussion some other time?'

'No. Jess, do you agree that this is the case?'

'What are you asking, exactly?'

'Even in these so-called "liberated" times, why do women still insist on assuming such a passive role in male/female relations?'

'You're talking bimbos, not feminists,' I retorted.

'Oh yeah? I'm guessing that you would classify yourself as a feminist, Jess. So how many times have you been the one to start something happening with a guy?'

'Me?' The conversation had taken a decidedly personal turn for the worse.

Max stood there, waiting for an answer.

'I've got better things to do with my life,' I said, shrugging my shoulders.

'Fine! Sorry to interrupt,' he snapped, disappearing again into the kitchen.

I tried to refocus my attention back on the computer screen but instead just sat there, gazing vacantly into space and wondering why he had become so confrontational.

'I can't hear your fingers tapping on the keyboard,' Max called.

'I've finished,' I answered to the wall.

'Liar.'

There was silence for another few minutes. Then I heard him sigh.

'This is silly,' he muttered, but loud enough for me to hear.

'What happened?'

'I'm not sure, but it wasn't good.'

I got up and went into the kitchen.

'Perhaps you're right,' I said, joining him at the table. 'Maybe women don't take the initiative because they're worried about being rejected.'

'But is it any easier for us?'

I had to acknowledge that he had a point.

'I tell you, Jess, a guy can't win either way. For example, if you like someone and launch yourself at her, you're instantly branded a sleaze-bag if she doesn't feel the same way about you. So you decide not to launch, but if she does happen to like you, chances are that you'll never find this out, because she's still doing the traditional thing and expecting you to make the first move.'

Max finished his little lecture and looked apprehensively at me. Suddenly I understood. We weren't actually having a theoretical debate; he was talking about us. I immediately resolved on a course of action: avoidance, followed by distraction.

'Hey, after my work is done, let's go and shoot a few rounds of pool. Will that cheer you up?'

Max sighed heavily and conceded defeat by picking up his newspaper again. Feeling enormously relieved, I made my escape back to the computer. I'd dodged a bullet and had managed to avert Failed Relationship #4. Now able to give my full attention to the report, I finished it in record time. I switched off the computer and marched into the kitchen where Max was making a cup of coffee, his back turned. As he reached up for the jar on the shelf, I caught a glimpse of a small strip of naked skin between his t-shirt and jeans. I walked behind him to grab a cup out of the sink and instead, to my absolute horror, found myself putting my arms around his exposed waist.

'Sorry, do you want a coffee too?' he asked.

I had lost the power of speech, appalled at what I was doing.

Max began to move to the left to grab the milk out of the fridge and so I let go, but his hands gently returned my arms to his waist. He made a coffee for me and then turned around.

'Here.'

He looked me full in the face, his eyebrows raised in a question. I took the cup from him and put it down on the bench.

'Okay. You win,' I finally said and kissed him lightly on the lips.

'That's it?'

'You're expecting sex on the kitchen floor?'

'Not exactly. My housemates are due back soon,' he grinned.

'Can we go and get a pizza? I'm starving.'

As we walked to where my car was parked, he held my hand, as if we were a couple of fifteen-year-olds. I wondered what the hell I'd done. Was I out of my mind? I had crossed the line and engaged with the enemy, no question about it, and I knew that there was no going back. Shit!

HEADING NOWHERE FAST
(Nikki)

It felt like mega-years since I'd last been to The Purple Crush, but the place hadn't changed one iota. Same old lights hanging low over the tables, the same scuffed green felt and the same crappy pool cues that needed constant chalking.

'Happy New Year!' said Max when he and Jess arrived.

'Yeah, right.'

'Surely this one will be better for you,' Jess put in.

'Want to make a bet?'

'What's been happening?'

'Nothing.'

Jess swapped looks with Max.

'How was Christmas?' she asked as Max got up and left us.

'A goddamn laugh a minute.'

'How come?'

'No reason.'

'Did Aunty Lil come over for Christmas lunch?'

'You mean That-Woman-Who-Is-Not-My-Mother.'

'Did she?'

'Nah, she's away.'

'Whereabouts?'

'How should I know?'

Max put a can of Coke down in front of me.

'So was it just you and your parents?'

'It was our turn to have dear old Grandma and all the rest.'

'You're joking.'

'I didn't hang around. Why should I?'

'So what did you do?'

'I left before they came and just wandered around the streets for a few hours.'

'They let you miss lunch?'

'I told them that I've become a vegetarian.'

'Hey, that's great!' said Daniel, suddenly arriving at our table with Amanda. 'I'm a vegetarian, and have been my entire life.'

'Your parents don't eat meat? Not even my parents are *that* weird,' said Jess.

'Ha! What else would you expect from Mr and Mrs Normal?'

'Nikki, why are you . . .' Max began, but copped a look from Jess. 'So are we talking or playing today?'

'I'm ready,' said Daniel. 'Hey, wait. There's too many of us.'

'Count me out.'

'What?'

Everyone stared at me.

'Headache.'

'Come on,' Jess said. 'I haven't beaten you for ages. You can't spoil my fun like this.'

'I couldn't care less. Go and smash someone else.'

'Nikki, please don't be like this,' she pleaded, but I just walked away.

The game started with Jess and Max playing against Daniel and Amanda. Two happy little couples. Jess kept glancing over in my direction. What the hell was the matter with her? I moved to a far corner and sat down on the couch, facing the wall.

Lil was being completely gutless. She was in hiding somewhere on the Gold Coast, presumably thinking that it would all blow over if enough time had passed. Seriously, that woman was dumber than dogshit. For now that I knew the truth, there was no way that we could continue on per normal. Lil *did* give birth to me. I *was* adopted by my aunt and uncle. And I *did* find out about it. None of these facts were miraculously going to change.

'You okay?' Jess asked, appearing in front of me.

'Yes. Why wouldn't I be?'

When she walked off, I sighed. Maybe I was like one of those pathetic cabbage patch kids, the kind that everyone feels sorry for because it comes with adoption papers. When I was growing up, the little girl next-door had one and without a doubt, it was the ugliest doll that I'd ever seen. And why was such a goddamn fuss made about its origins? News flash: all dolls come from factories, even cabbage patch kids! It was such bullshit.

Right from the start, I'd been aware that I was different. Everyone else at school had real families, complete with brothers and sisters. There was only one other exception – Sarah. Her parents were so old when they had her that they couldn't have any more kids, so she remained an only child. She was considered to be totally weird and was shunned, except when it was her birthday. Then everyone wanted to be her friend because at her birthday parties, there were humungous lolly bags and a jumping castle, so it was important to score an invite. Yet I didn't have a brother or a sister, and I wasn't given any fancy birthday parties. All I had was a couple of people who pretended to be my parents but who actually weren't.

I had also been fed a whole load of crap about my bad genes, as if I'd been born with some type of inherited, major genetic fault. Like some rotten apple that was going to spoil the whole box. Or a virus that had snuck onto the computer and could crash the entire system. That was me. Yet now I had discovered that I was an actual blood relative, with the same blood that ran through the Johnstone side of the family . . . and yet my very own mother refused to acknowledge the truth of this!

I looked around to see that the game of pool was over. Jess and Max had won – no surprise there. The happy little foursome came over to where I was sitting and Jess plonked herself down beside me. I wished that I'd thought earlier to put my bag on the seat, so that there wouldn't have been any room for her.

'What did you get up to on New Year's Eve?' she asked.

'Oh, the usual. I had so many parties to go to that I didn't get home until February. Man, what a rage.'

They all stared at me.

'What are you talking about? It's still only January,' said Daniel.

'One of my cousins had a big party,' Amanda butted in. 'I'm sorry that I didn't invite you.'

'I thought that you people celebrate New Year later on,' I said, with a snort.

I felt a sharp elbow in my ribs and Jess snapped, 'That's Chinese New Year, you idiot.'

'Well, how should I know?'

The whole lot of them gawked at me again. It was obviously Dump-on-Nikki Day.

'In fact,' Amanda said, 'Vietnamese people do celebrate a Lunar New Year as well. Anyway, what about you, Max? What did you do?'

'After trying to extricate Jess from her books and failing, I went to Lisa's party.'

'Lisa from the Student Union? How come you scored an invite to that?'

'Through me,' replied Daniel. 'Lisa thinks he's pretty hot – she was all over him at the party.'

'Really?'

'Yeah, until she got nowhere and then switched her attentions to you,' Max reminded Daniel.

'She was very drunk by that stage, mate!'

'Then what happened?'

The pair of them laughed. 'Don't know. We split and went back to Daniel's place.'

'Oh?'

'Yeah, we talked till dawn.'

'Though I think that the beer we were drinking may have done most of the talking!'

The two guys smirked at each other, like they were the best buddies in the world.

'Oh, please,' I said, 'give me a bucket!' I made throwing-up noises.

Jess elbowed me again – she was really getting on my nerves. I stood up and said that I had to go. Nobody tried to stop me.

Out on the street, I made the decision to never play pool again. I was sick to death of losing all the time. Jess was so bloody competitive and always had to win . . . and did. She was smart and beautiful, had a real family and was a brilliant pool player. She was a born winner, whereas I was born a complete loser. Why was I even trying to beat her? Did I honestly believe that was going to happen? Ha! I'd never stood a chance against her; I just hadn't realised it.

For I was a failure, a dud, a waste of space. I could do nothing right. In fact, I was the exact opposite of that guy called Midas – everything I touched turned to shit. I couldn't even manage to fix my own car. Ever since the accident, The Beast kept stalling, after idling for only a few minutes. I had absolutely no idea why, although I'd been trying for ages to work it out. And where was Daniel? Why wasn't he helping me? After Amanda had showed up, I hadn't seen him for dust. He was always chasing after her, following behind like some pathetic love-sick puppy, while I'd obviously been forgotten.

So I gave up trying to get The Beast back on the road and there he remained, in the parking lot behind the garage. I thought about throwing a tarp over him, but decided not to bother. After all, what did it matter if the paint job got damaged?

One day I arrived home from work to find Aunty Rose's Ford Laser parked in the driveway. However I found not only Aunty Rose sitting at our kitchen table, but also That-Woman-Who-Is-Not-My-Mother. I instantly marched into my bedroom to listen to some music, until I was interrupted by loud banging on the door. I was being called for dinner. I walked into the dining room, sat down and picked up my knife and fork.

'You're back,' I said, without looking at her.

'Yes, but Edna has stayed on for an extra week. We both absolutely love the Gold Coast and we've found a terrific beachfront apartment. Next time you'll have to come up for a visit.

'I'd rather stab myself in the eye with a sharp stick,' I thought to myself.

They continued on discussing the marvels of the Gold Coast amongst themselves, while I scoffed down my food as quickly as I could.

'May I please be excused.'

'Of course not,' growled my father.

'How's your apprenticeship going? What's your news, Nicola?'

I looked up and across the table to glare at That-Woman-Who-Is-Not-My-Mother. She was grinning back, expectantly.

'My news? Well, there's some very old news that you may be interested in,' I said and watched her lower her gaze.

'Do you know that Nikki had a car accident?' piped up my mother.

'Oh no. That's dreadful. What happened?'

I shrugged my shoulders in reply, and the conversation returned to the Gold Coast. I sat there, staring at my empty plate, waiting for the moment I could make my escape. All of a sudden, I became aware that someone was standing right beside me.

'Aunty Rose's car is making a very strange noise,' that woman was whispering. 'You need to take a look.' She grabbed the keys from her sister and was just about to walk out the door, when she turned around to see me still seated. 'Hurry up,' she ordered, and so I slowly got to my feet and followed her outside.

What on earth had gone wrong with the Ford Laser? I'd thoroughly checked it over before advising Aunty Rose to buy it. What could I have possibly overlooked? Had I stuffed up again? I popped the bonnet, turned on the engine and examined everything closely, but all seemed to be in good working order.

'What sort of noise is it making?'

'I think it was coming from the back.'

'Hmm. Maybe the muffler. But it's sounding okay now.'

I studied underneath the car.

'It looks fine to me.'

'Let's go for a drive and see if the noise returns,' she suggested.

I got into the passenger seat, she backed out of the driveway and when we turned into Chester St, she said,

'Nicola, you have to stop behaving like this.'

Shit. I'd been ambushed. I couldn't get out of a moving car.

'Ivy is your mother. That's what she knows. In fact, that's *all* she knows.'

'No,' I replied. 'What I know is that *you* are my mother. And by the way, who's my goddamn father?'

I saw her hands tighten on the steering wheel.

'Do you want to destroy your mother?'

'What's she got to do with it? Tell me about my birth!'

'I've said all that I need to say.'

'But you've told me nothing!'

She drove back without saying another word, her eyes firmly fixed straight ahead. The minute we were in the driveway again, she wrenched the handbrake on before leaping out of the car.

'You're a bloody coward!' I yelled after her, but she'd already disappeared into the house.

That night, I was way too furious to sleep. Sometime in the early hours of the morning, I realised that I wasn't going to get anywhere with That-Woman-Who-Is-Not-My-Mother, and that I needed to seriously change direction. So the next evening I walked into the kitchen where my mother was doing her dinner prep and offered to help. She almost fell over from shock, but recovered enough to pass me a large bag of peas and a bowl. I wasted no time in kick-starting the conversation.

'So how did you come to adopt me?' I asked.

'Don't you remember the story? I've told you a million times.'

'Yes, but I want to hear it again.'

'After years and years of being on a waiting list, finally we got a call from the orphanage. They asked your father and me to come in immediately. And there you were, a tiny newborn, crying your eyes out in a bassinet. I picked you up but that made you scream even louder. However, when they gave—'

'I have a question,' I interrupted. 'What did Aunty Lil think of me? Er, and Aunty Rose?'

'They both thought you were marvellous. Though I never could get Rose to change your nappy,' she grumbled.

'And Aunty Lil did?'

'Hmm. Now that I think of it, probably she didn't either. She was away at Bible College in NSW, so she wasn't around for those first few years. And naturally your father was no help when it came to—'

'Bible College? Did she come and visit much?'

'From interstate? No, not at all. It was too far, but we talked for hours at a time on the phone.'

'Hmm. And did she mention a boyfriend?'

At this, she laughed. 'Lil? Don't be ridiculous. She was never interested in boys.'

'Are you saying that she was a lesbian?'

'A what? Of course not! How can you suggest such a dreadful thing? It was just that she was never keen to go on any dates. Rose and I did, but not Lil. Even as a teenager, she'd insist that she was already in love . . . with God, and that He was all she needed.'

Well, that was her first big fat lie. What am I – a product of an immaculate conception? I don't think so! Obviously devout old Lily had cheated on God . . . but who the hell with?

'Surely there must have been some guy,' I said aloud.

'No. Never, and she was perfectly happy. Unlike poor Rose. When she was jilted at the altar, she cried for days and days. I don't think that she ever got over it, and there was never another suitor.'

What was this – a third-rate soap opera? But she was already continuing on.

'So that left just little old me, and even though I'm the youngest, I'm the only one who got married and had my own family,' she said, grinning like a Cheshire cat.

Of course I'd heard her say this before, because it was one of her favourite lines. But now I knew it for what it was – complete and utter crap! I looked at this woman, who was my real aunt and who had no clue that it was her sister who'd actually had a child. I sighed, and brought our discussion back to the topic.

'Were you given a choice of babies?'

'No. We'd been specially selected to be your parents.'

'Really? Who by?'

'Matron Robinson. She was in charge of the whole orphanage. Amazingly, she'd gone to school with Lily and so—'

'Wait a minute. The matron of the orphanage was an old school friend of Aunty Lil's?'

'Yes, wasn't that a stroke of luck? This is why she took a particular interest in our situation, and was so good to us.'

Luck or a set-up? My money was on the second.

'Apparently by then, we were too old to adopt, but nobody had bothered to tell us. Matron Robinson made an exception for your father and me because she'd decided that you were the ideal little baby for us.'

Ha! I snorted to myself. Sucked in, big time!

'Oh no!' she suddenly said, grabbing my bowl. 'You've shelled the whole week's supply of peas! You were only meant to do tonight's. Ah well, here's some potatoes to peel.'

But I shook my head. 'I can't,' I mumbled and jumped off my stool.

Escaping into my bedroom, I lay down on my bed, my thoughts in a whirl. What a lying, cunning, despicable person Lily was. She had managed to keep her pregnancy, and my birth, a complete secret from everyone, by cloistering herself away at bloody Bible College. It was the perfect cover. And how convenient it was for her that her old school buddy was a matron of an orphanage, so that her shame could be instantly whisked away and palmed off onto her unsuspecting, younger but married sister. Lily got to keep her oh-so-pious reputation, by getting rid of me.

As if by magic, she had made the truth completely disappear. It was as if there was never a man in her life, or a baby. Vanished in a puff of smoke! A shocking secret that not even her sisters knew. But I knew, because I happened to be the secret. I was that embarrassing skeleton in the cupboard.

I took the pillow out from under my head and punched it. I had to bust out of the closet . . . but how? I still had a lot to figure out.

WHAT THE HELL IS GOING ON?
(Jess)

Nikki shouted so loudly at me that others in the cafeteria turned to stare.

'You have absolutely no idea!' she snapped.

'Hey, there's no need to get upset,' I told her. 'I'm just trying to explain that you're wasting your time going over the same old ground. It happened in the past. Aunty Lil made a decision eighteen years ago and now you simply have to accept it, and move on.'

'Move on? Everything's so goddamn simple and easy for you, isn't it!' she sneered, banging her Coke can down hard on the table.

I glared at her. What did she know about my life? Had it been easy for me as a kid when my parents separated? What about being saddled with the ridiculous name Karma? No. I'd had to make a massive effort to break free from my past and create a new, independent future for myself.

'Nikki, you have a choice,' I said, as calmly as I could. 'It's your life and it's up to you, and you alone, to make it whatever you want.'

'No! It wasn't my choice to be thrown away by my mother!'

To my relief, Amanda appeared and sat down at our table.

'What's going on? How come you two are here and not at The Purple Crush?'

'One of us,' I replied, 'has decided that she no longer wants to play pool.' Deliberately not looking at Nikki, I quickly added, 'So what's up with you?'

Amanda groaned. 'My mother lost her job yesterday.'

'That's terrible,' I said. 'What was the job?'

'She was cleaning offices in the city, although actually she's a teacher.'

'What do you mean?'

'She taught for fifteen years in a primary school.'

'Back in Vietnam?'

Amanda nodded. 'As a cleaner, she wasn't bringing home nearly the money she used to make, and now she doesn't even have that any more. Poor Mum.'

'Does your father work?'

'Yes, he drives taxis, but the money that he earns isn't enough to keep my little sister at her Catholic girls' school. Dad used to be a dentist and we lived a comfortable, middle-class life in Vietnam, but here we can't afford anything. I don't know what we're going to do.'

Nikki suddenly exhaled noisily and said, 'So he should get a job as a dentist. Problem solved.'

'Dentistry qualifications from Vietnam aren't recognised in Australia, and neither are teaching qualifications.'

'Well, they should be grateful for a new start in the good old lucky country.'

'Some start,' Amanda muttered and pushed her chair back. 'Do either of you want anything?'

Nikki and I shook our heads, and Amanda walked across to the food counter to take her place in the queue.

'She's up herself, isn't she,' Nikki said.

'You're talking about Amanda?'

'Yeah. She reckons that she's so much better than everyone else.'

'No, she doesn't. Why are you saying this? What's wrong with you today?'

'You didn't notice how she just happened to mention that her father's a dentist and her mother's a teacher? Except that they aren't, not really.'

'She was explaining how different things are for her family in Australia. And difficult.'

'Whatever. Anyway, she isn't very pretty, is she.'

'Seriously? You want to discuss how pretty she is? You care about this? Why does her appearance matter?'

'Because it matters to a lot of people.'

'Which people?'

'Males.'

'Ha! Since when did you decide that males are part of the human race?'

But Nikki was not to be diverted. 'Guys only check out the spunks. If you're not a babe, they walk right past you, like you're not even there.'

At that point, Amanda arrived back at the table and there was an awkward silence, which she broke. 'So what are we talking about?' she asked.

'Nothing,' Nikki mumbled.

'Come on.'

'Actually,' I said, 'we were discussing the way that guys focus all their attention on attractive women. Do you think that's true?'

Amanda poured sugar into her tea and stirred it slowly with a plastic spoon, considering the question.

'I don't think it's that straight-forward,' she finally said. 'There are certain things that seem to set them off. For instance, you can be in the middle of a great conversation with some intelligent guy but if a woman walks past with large breasts or wearing a short skirt, he immediately becomes a leering zombie who can't string two words together.'

'I know exactly what you mean. Why is this?'

'Stop!' Nikki broke in loudly, shaking her head. 'This isn't funny at all!'

'What?' I said. We hadn't been laughing.

'Anyway,' she addressed Amanda, 'girls like you shouldn't play the dumb bimbo so that you can get the guy you want!'

'Hang on, that isn't fair—' I began, but this time she had gone too far, even for the usually good-natured Amanda.

'You're calling me a "dumb bimbo", Nikki?' she asked, jumping to her feet.

'I call it how I see it.'

'This is absurd. What is your problem?'

'You're the problem! You're such a goddamn flirt!'

Amanda stared down at Nikki for a few seconds.

'You know perfectly well that this isn't true. So is this about Daniel?'

'Daniel? What's he got to do with this?'

'Bitch-fight!' someone nearby called out. 'Fan-bloody-tastic!'

Horrified, I immediately instructed Nikki and Amanda to follow me, and shepherded them out of the cafeteria and into the toilets downstairs. Once there, Nikki hoisted herself onto the washbasin bench while Amanda went to stand in a far corner of the room, with her back to us.

'Amanda?'

She turned around and to my surprise, I saw that tears were streaming down her face.

'Sorry,' she said. 'I always cry when I'm angry. Ridiculous, I know.' She roughly brushed the tears away with her sleeve.

'What the hell do you have to be angry about?' Nikki shouted.

'You've been treating me like absolute crap for ages, and I've had a gutful.'

'No! It's me who's had a gutful!'

'If this is about Daniel, then blame him for whatever he's doing, or not doing! Not me. I'm not responsible for Daniel's behaviour.'

'There you go again! You talk about Daniel all the time. It makes me want to puke!'

'You want to puke because you're jealous! Wake up to yourself, for Christ's sake!'

Nikki stormed into a cubicle and slammed the door shut.

'Nikki?' I called.

No reply.

'Do you think that Daniel is interested in Amanda?'

'How would I know!'

'Yes or no?'

'I couldn't care less about Daniel!'

'So what's this all about?'

'It's *her*. She's so sleazy. Real slime-bucket stuff.'

'That's bullshit!' Amanda shouted.

'No it isn't! When you locked your keys in the car, you were all over Daniel like a rash! Hugging him non-stop when he handed over the keys.'

'And do you remember why I was in such a state? Because I didn't want to miss my date with Tristan. Remember him, you idiot?'

'You could've asked me to help. I could've got those keys out much quicker than Daniel did.'

'I didn't care *who* got them out, as long as I made it home by six.'

'Then what about the time when you and he went to the movies?'

'So what?' Amanda cried. 'We both wanted to see the same movie. Is there a law against it? I've gone to the movies with you and I haven't been accused of trying to race *you* off.'

There was a bit of a pause.

'Once and for all, I'm not after Daniel.'

'So you think you're too good for him, do you?' Nikki yelled.

'Oh, for God's sake!'

We could hear Nikki banging her fist against the wall. Amanda closed her eyes and sighed deeply. She then said over the din, 'Do you know what makes me really mad about all of this?'

The banging stopped.

'That you believe I would go after the same guy you like. What kind of low-life do you think I am?'

No sound came from behind the closed door.

'Nikki! Come out!' I ordered.

'Piss off!'

Amanda looked at me and I shook my head. I knew Nikki. Even if she was starting to see reason, which I frankly doubted, it wasn't likely that she was going to leap out of the cubicle and apologise. It just wasn't her style. I decided that it was better to leave her alone to cool off, and perhaps eventually she would come to her senses. I gestured towards the door but Amanda hadn't finished.

'One last thing, Nikki,' she said quietly. 'I haven't betrayed you, not one iota. However, you have been *the worst friend* I've ever had in my life!' She then marched out of the toilets, with me trailing behind.

After this, Nikki stopped coming to TAFE. None of us heard from her, not even Daniel. Two weeks went past. I thought about ringing her but didn't end up calling, because around this time I realised that Nikki wasn't my only problem. Max too had become a veritable thorn in my side. For he was insisting that we spend every single night together, and seemed to take it for granted that he would eventually move into my place. Clearly he was making a myriad of assumptions about me, and about our relationship. I needed to act, and fast. I decided on a simple yet effective solution: to shift my usual daytime work hours at the Student Union to evenings. This way I knew that I could easily dodge Max, with the additional bonus of completing some overdue tasks.

The following Monday I had worked for four hours straight on the financial procedures review before I decided to call it a night, even though it was only 9:10 pm. I had planned to finish it but realised that my concentration was already starting to flag. I switched off the computer, checked that the door leading to the smoke detector was closed and lit a cigarette.

I leant back in my chair and looked around. During the day the Student Union office was crammed full of people, noise and activity, but now, in the stillness of the evening, I became aware of the untidy desks, the twisted telephone cords and the unwashed coffee cups. The carpet was littered with small, white paper circles which was a sure sign that Roger, who had a passion for filing things in ring folders, had been there that day. Lisa too had obviously been around, judging by the crumpled-up tissues in one of the waste paper baskets, as she attempted to hide her revolting Nicorette chewing gum habit. Everywhere I looked, I saw evidence of the office's inhabitants and the by-products of their activities.

Suddenly I heard footsteps and then a key being turned in the lock. I had just enough time to butt out my cigarette and put the saucer into a nearby drawer.

'So I said that they . . .' I watched as Maria, the cleaner, propped open the door with a wheelie bin. 'Sweet mother of Jesus!' she cried out, brandishing a duster in my direction. 'Jess! You scared me half to death!'

Del, her sister, appeared beside her. 'And what do you think you're doing here at this time of night? Haven't you got a home to go to?'

'I'm just about to leave.'

'And what's this I can smell?' Del had missed her calling in life; she had the natural skills of a customs sniffer dog.

'Oh dear. Is there a bad smell in here? Do you think it could be all these old coffee cups?' I examined the inside of a nearby mug and wrinkled my nose.

'Who's been smoking?' Del speaks with a strong Italian accent; nevertheless, she somehow manages to sound exactly like my mother.

'Could've been Jason. I'll have a word with him if you like.'

She held her hand out, expectantly. I sighed, opened the drawer and handed over my ashtray.

She rolled her eyes in disapproval. 'A smart girl like you doesn't understand that there's no smoking in this place? You can't read the big signs everywhere? Besides, I've told you before, how are you going to get a man if you stink like a chimney? They don't like it, you know.'

'Don't tell me that or I'll never even think about quitting.'

'You don't want a man?'

'Haven't you heard that "a woman needs a man like a fish needs a bicycle"?'

'Cheeky thing!' Maria said and shook her head, but forgot to hide her smile. The two women began emptying the waste paper baskets.

'And a man certainly doesn't want a smarty-pants for a wife,' added Del.

'So how does your husband manage?'

'Sometimes,' she winked, 'a man has to settle for what he can get.'

We both laughed and then she pulled her mouth down into a frown while pointing at her watch.

'Okay, okay, I'm going!' I grumbled.

Maria wheeled the rubbish bin out the door. 'If you're still here by the time we come back to vacuum, then . . .'

'Bye!' I shouted. I found my backpack and dashed out in three seconds flat.

As they unlocked the door to the next lot of offices, I made my way up the stairs. A wave of exhaustion engulfed me and I realised that I should have left hours ago. I tried to remember what I had eaten for lunch, but drew a blank. Perhaps I'd had nothing? It occurred to me that I needed to eat more regularly and to generally take better care of my health. Priority #1 for tomorrow, I decided, would be to come up with a health improvement plan. Maybe I could even start thinking about cutting down the number of cigarettes I smoked each day. The money I'd save would mean that I could afford to buy that book on—

'You're working very late again,' a voice said, breaking across my thoughts.

I became aware of a man, slouching against the wall of the corridor, just a little ahead of me. I examined his face – nondescript brown eyes, small nose, bad skin. I guessed his age to be about thirty by the lines around his eyes. Still unable to place him, I nodded politely. He obviously knew who I was. A security guy, perhaps? Or a new cleaner?

'It's been a long day,' I replied and walked past him.

'You look tired.'

'Sure am. See you,' I mumbled over my shoulder.

I continued on my way down the seemingly endless corridor. I groaned when I thought of the distance to the car park. I wished that cars could turn themselves on and drive up when you whistle . . .

and then I laughed at myself. I was so exhausted that I was becoming silly.

I heard thudding footsteps behind me and turned to find the security guy walking briskly towards me.

'You dropped this,' he called.

He halted directly in front of me and slowly uncurled the fingers of his left hand, to display a knife. I stood there, wondering what the hell a knife was doing in the palm of his outstretched hand.

'It's mine,' he whispered.

I looked up. He was grinning at me.

'I might decide to use it.'

I took a step backwards, my heart beginning to pound. I watched his grin disappear from his face. He moved forward.

'Now don't you scream, little girlie,' he said.

I stood there, paralysed, caught in the venom of his eyes.

'Take off your shirt, slut!' he ordered, lowering his eyes to stare at my breasts. He was so close that I could see the beads of sweat breaking through the hair follicles on his scalp. He slowly raised the knife, breathing heavily. With one hand, he held my shirt out and with the other, he began to slice.

'Please don't hurt me,' I whimpered.

The man laughed and kept hacking. I felt my shirt dissolve into fragments as it was cut and looking down, I saw that he had exposed my breasts through two ragged holes.

'I'll teach you, bitch!' he suddenly shouted. 'Lie down. NOW!' He was undoing his belt, unzipping his fly.

I didn't move so he pushed me onto the floor.

'Pretending to play hard to get, are you? But I know your type. Soon you'll be screaming for more, begging for it.'

I jammed my eyes shut. My whole body was shaking. I waited. Nothing happened. I looked up to see him standing above me, one hand around a limp penis.

'This is your fault, you fucking whore!'

I watched as he aimed his urine at my face. My arms encircled my head, too late, and I wondered if I was going to vomit.

'HEY!' came a shout. 'What's going on here?'

There was the sound of people running.

'Is that you, Jess?' a voice said.

'What's happened? Oh my God. Del, call the police. And an ambulance. Jess, Jess, are you hurt?' I could feel gentle hands touching my shoulders. I slowly managed to uncurl and sit up.

Maria was standing there. I blinked and looked around. The man had disappeared. I tried to speak, but no sound came out. Maria helped me stand up. She was crying softly and stroking my hair.

'We'll get you to a hospital straight away.'

Someone rushed up.

'The ambulance will be here any minute.' It was Del. 'I told them to come to the side entrance. You can walk a little bit?'

'We'll help you.' Maria and Del began walking slowly, holding me firmly between them.

'But I don't want to go to hospital,' I whispered.

'You need to see a doctor.'

'I'm not hurt,' I mumbled.

'Don't be ridiculous. You're in shock.'

'I just need to rest for a minute.'

'Come on, put one foot in front of the other,' Del insisted and kept propelling me by the elbow.

I wrenched my arm out of her grasp.

'No!'

I listened as my shout echoed down the long expanse of corridor. Then I filled my lungs with air again.

'NO!' I screamed, and began to sob.

The trip in the ambulance passed in a blur. I was transferred into a hospital cubicle and Maria held my hand as I was examined, murmuring 'You'll be okay,' over and over again. Later on, there were two policewomen standing above me, asking questions. There was a lot of crying; some of it could have been mine.

Eventually I was walked through the hospital corridors by my mother, who had materialised at some stage during the night. She loaded me into her car and I gazed out of the window as we passed through the empty streets. I looked at my watch, and was surprised by the time. I had assumed it to be a lot later.

My mother put me into my old bed and tucked me in, as if I were a child. I switched off the bedside light. But the second that I had closed my eyes, the man's face flashed before me. I leapt up and turned the light back on.

Naturally, I'd had a terrible fright. If Maria and Del hadn't shown up . . . but I shook my head firmly. I knew that it was a mistake to dwell on the 'what ifs' and so I tried to think of something else. It didn't work. Why did that man have a knife? Was it simply to scare me, or had he intended to kill me with it? I recalled the expression on his face and instantaneously knew that he had been capable of anything.

I got out of bed to grab *The Secret Garden*, one of my favourite books when I was a child. However I only made it to the second page. Who was that guy? Did I know him? Did he know me? Why did he hate me so much? What had I ever done to him? Did he hate all women and I'd just happened to be at the wrong place at the wrong time? Or had he singled me out especially? Had he been waiting in that corridor for me? Would he have left me alone if I hadn't spoken to him? Why hadn't I walked straight past him, without a word?

Nothing was working. I couldn't block out his face or silence his voice. Every moment replayed itself, in vivid slow-motion detail. Why had I just stood there, letting him do those things to me, like a lamb to the slaughter? Why hadn't I tried to stop him? Why, at the very least, had I made no real effort to escape? Or even to shout for help? Would it have made things worse if I had tried? My feeble attempts at begging seemed to have only succeeded in spurring him on. Perhaps, I thought, some kind of survival instinct had guided me not to oppose him, that somehow I'd known that compliance was the best course of action.

Seriously? Who the hell was I trying to kid? Survival instinct? Course of action? I had been absolutely terrified and that was why I hadn't acted. This was the simple truth. I had felt powerless and vulnerable, immobilised by my own fear, and by the strength of his hatred. When confronted by an attacker, I had frozen. Me! I could scarcely believe it.

I decided to have a bath, even though I'd had a thorough wash at the hospital. But as I lay in the hot steaming water, I could hardly bear to look at my exposed body. I grabbed a cloth from the shower cubicle, covered myself with soap and began to scrub. I wondered if I would ever feel clean again.

Eventually I returned to my bed and lay there with my hands wedged tightly between my thighs. This time I didn't turn off the bedside light. As a child, I'd never been scared of the dark but that night, as a twenty-one-year-old woman, I learnt to be afraid.

MAKING A COUPLE OF U-TURNS
(Nikki)

I couldn't find the doorbell, so I banged as hard as I could on the solid wooden door. All of a sudden it opened and there in the doorway stood Jess. I felt enormously relieved.

'Oh Jess. Are you okay?'

'Why wouldn't I be?'

'Daniel told me what happened. It sounded really terrible.'

She just shrugged her shoulders.

'Can I come in?'

'If you must.'

'What a shocker of a drive!' I said as I followed her into the house. 'This place is totally out in the sticks, isn't it? Why don't they seal any of the roads?'

'How the hell did you find me?'

'When I couldn't get hold of you on the phone, I went over to your sister's flat and she gave me this address.'

A hippy-looking woman wandered into the room. She smiled at me and there was a strange pause.

'This is Kate,' Jess finally muttered.

'Who?'

'My mother.'

I stared at her. Her mother? She didn't look anything like what I'd imagined.

'Hi, I'm Nikki.'

'Can I get you a peppermint tea?'

'A what? I'd like a Coke, please.'

'I'm afraid I don't have Coke. What about a coffee?'

'Yeah, that'd be good.'

She disappeared and I turned back to Jess.

'Well? What happened?'

She didn't reply.

'Come on.'

'A man bailed me up in the corridor at TAFE and then pissed on me. End of story.'

'Yeah, but—'

'I wasn't raped. He didn't stab me. In fact, he didn't even hit me,' she snapped, before adding, 'Nikki, I really wish you'd leave.'

I stared at Jess, who was scowling back at me. Then suddenly it struck me like a bolt of lightning – she was angry with me and honestly, who could blame her?

'Jess, I'm so sorry,' I said. 'I know that I've been an absolute arsehole lately.'

She looked a bit surprised.

'I should never have taken my crap out on you,' I went on, 'especially when you were trying to help.'

'Doesn't matter.'

'Not true, it does matter. You've been incredibly good to me and I've been an ungrateful little turd.'

'But I didn't DO anything!' she said loudly.

'Bullshit! You've done heaps! I wouldn't have got my licence without you and—'

'NO! You don't get it!' She began to pace around the room. 'I didn't run, I didn't yell, I didn't even try to stop him. I didn't put up any kind of fight.'

It took me a few seconds to realise that we were no longer talking about her and me.

'Yeah, but was there anything you could've done? It might have made things worse if you'd struggled.'

She halted, mid-stride, before marching over to me.

'I did nothing! NOTHING!' she screamed into my face.

'Do you take sugar, Nikki?' began Jess's mother, entering the room. 'I'm afraid we only have—'

But before she could finish, Jess burst into tears.

Kate immediately got rid of the tray and put her arms around her daughter but was instantly pushed away.

'Why didn't you warn me?' Jess yelled.

'Darling, what are you talking about?'

'Why didn't you tell me that this could happen?'

Again her mother tried to hug her and was rejected.

'You should have prepared me,' Jess continued. 'You made me too trusting of other people.'

Kate moved forward and grabbed her daughter by the shoulders. 'Listen to me,' she said. 'I raised you and your sister to become strong, independent women who could go anywhere, do anything and be whoever you wanted to be. Not two little nervous Nellies.'

'But I could've been hurt,' Jess whimpered, like a little kid.

Her mother's face crumpled. 'I know,' she said softly and pulled Jess in close. I think they were both crying.

I stood silently where I was, looking at the floor. I tried to remember the last time that my mother had hugged me, and couldn't, which made me want to cry too. Eventually Jess was put into a chair and her mother went out to make some fresh coffee. I sat down too.

'Hey, it wasn't your mother's fault,' I said.

She nodded slightly.

'And it wasn't your fault either.'

She looked at me then.

'Nothing you did or didn't do made that dickhead behave the way he did,' I persisted.

'I know that.'

'So why are you beating yourself up?'

'I'm not.'

'Yeah, right,' I said, and there was silence for a few minutes.

Suddenly, from out of nowhere, I had a flashback of a shocking incident of my own.

'Jess, I want to tell you something that I've never told anybody. Maybe it's related, maybe it isn't.'

I could see that she was listening, so I continued.

'On my fourteenth birthday, dear old Grandma explained to me that I should've been drowned at birth and what a terrible shame it was for everyone that I was still alive. Naturally this made me feel like a million bucks, so later that night I grabbed a bottle of Bundy Rum from the liquor cabinet and off I went in my car—'

'Hang on a minute. Whose car?'

'Mine. I was fixing up a Beetle, though I have no idea why. Those cars are only good for scrap metal!'

'At fourteen?'

'I'd bought it super cheap from a neighbour when I was twelve.'

'You're joking.'

'Can I get back to the story?'

'Sorry. Go on.'

'I sat in the car for a while, drinking and bawling my eyes out. I decided that I needed to kill myself, so when—'

'What?'

'You heard me. So when I was very drunk, I smashed through a barricade and drove into a nearby park. I flew full pelt down a steep hill, eventually smacking into a tree right down at the bottom.'

'Were you hurt?'

'No, I was fine although the car was a mangled wreck,' I said, taking a coffee from Kate. 'But that night was like some kind of weird turning point for me.'

'How?'

'When I staggered back up the hill, I promised myself that never again would I stand back and let someone treat me like a piece of shit. Nobody, and I mean nobody, has that right. Not Grandma, not another apprentice and certainly not some random goddamn wannabe rapist.'

Jess sighed. 'I just wish that I hadn't felt so terrified.'

'Of course you were terrified! That dickhead had a knife! Jess, don't get me wrong. What you went through was appalling. But what's even worse is the way these arseholes mess with our heads.'

'What do you mean?'

'I believed Grandma when she said that I was the lowest scum on earth, so I actually thought I was doing the world a favour by killing myself! But hitting that tree knocked some sense into me, because instantly I understood that Grandma had been talking a whole heap of bullshit. It wasn't me who was disgusting. It was her!'

Jess nodded.

'Arseholes like Grandma and that guy like to think that they have some kind of power over us, but they don't. We're the ones in charge of our lives, not them. We make our own decisions and choices. Of course I can't stop Grandma from being who she is, but I can stop myself from buying into her crap. And I can choose to stand up for myself, against her.'

'Yes, you're a fighter. Whereas I'm not sure that I am.'

'You're kidding me, right? Who always has to win? You won't let anyone beat you.'

'Nikki, playing a game of pool is completely different.'

'I don't think so. There are winners and losers in this world and you, my friend, are a winner.'

'Am I?' she said. 'Frankly, I'm not certain about anything anymore.'

'Fair enough. And hey, who am I to talk? I'm the idiot who allowed Grandma to make me feel so bad that I almost didn't get my license! Lucky that I had you to bail me out.'

'And lucky that you didn't die in the crash.'

'Not luck exactly. It was more like a mistake.'

'Mistake?'

I hesitated. I didn't want to explain, but Jess was waiting expectantly.

'Er, I was so hammered that I didn't realise that I had my seatbelt on.'

'You were trying to kill yourself but you were wearing a seatbelt?'

'Yep.'

'Oops!' Jess said, with a little wink. 'Perhaps you didn't want to get in trouble with the law?'

'As an under-age driver without a license in an unregistered car, of course I didn't want to be sprung without a seat belt!'

We both chuckled.

'By the way,' I said, looking around, 'where's your father?'

Jess immediately turned her face away from me and didn't reply. Kate answered instead.

'Rob will be around later. He takes his son to music lessons on a Saturday morning.'

'I didn't realise that you've got a brother, Jess.'

But she'd clammed up and was examining her hands.

'Dylan is her half-brother. Rob lives with his new family, over on the next hill.'

'You're joking!'

Gobsmacked, I stared at Kate but she was looking at her daughter. There was a strange pause. Had I said something wrong?

'I'm sorry,' I said.

'What on earth for?'

That really confused me. Another embarrassing silence.

'I just didn't get around to mentioning it to her,' Jess muttered finally to her mother.

'What?' I didn't have a clue what was going on.

'Can we please change the subject?' Jess snapped, crossing her arms.

Kate frowned, but turned back to me. 'Anyway, Nikki,' she said, 'you must come around again, sometime when Rob's here. I know he'd love to meet you. We never get to meet our daughter's friends.'

'That'd be great.'

Jess stood up, and I realised that it was definitely now time to leave. On my way out, I gave her a friendly pat on the arm and she closed the door.

I drove home, my thoughts whirling around in my head. Nothing made any sense. Jess had lied to me about her family! She'd made out that she had a normal family, when she didn't at all. Her father didn't live with her mother plus he had other kids, and yet

Kate seemed to be okay about it. She'd even said 'we', meaning her and her ex-husband, as if they were still friends. So why was it such a problem for Jess and why had she lied about it?

Or had she? I thought back to our conversations and realised that she'd never actually lied. She'd just kept me in the dark. She hadn't mentioned that she had a sister, until she had to, when she moved into the flat after her break-up with Luke. Come to think of it, she'd never said a word about her parents, keeping them a big fat secret.

Suddenly I remembered that I'd forgotten to check the water in the radiator before taking off. Ever since Fred helped me get back on the road, The Beast had been losing water. I looked for a spot to pull over but there wasn't anywhere to stop. Fortunately the temperature gauge was indicating that there was no immediate problem, so I kept on driving until I found a petrol station.

I had to wait for the engine to cool down before I could unscrew the radiator cap, so I walked into the shop to kill some time. I examined the car magazines for a long while, before eventually grabbing a can of Coke out of the fridge and heading towards the cash register. I almost stopped dead in my tracks. For there, behind the counter, stood an Asian girl who reminded me instantly of Amanda. I quickly handed her the money and bolted outside.

Amanda. What the hell had happened there? Why had she insisted that I was jealous of her and Daniel? Was I? Did I like Daniel in that way? He and I were good friends, and had been for ages, but was there anything more than that? No, of course there wasn't. Especially since everyone in the world knew that Daniel was completely besotted with Amanda, not me. And who could blame him? Amanda had everything going for her, while I had nothing. That's what pissed me off the most.

I took a swig of Coke, and realised something. I was wrong. It wasn't Amanda who was annoying the crap out of me. It was Jess. Bloody Jess who had the terrific life and the great family. She was the winner at goddamn everything, not Amanda. If someone came up to me and offered me the choice of being either Jess or Amanda, it wouldn't take me a nanosecond to decide. I know exactly which one I'd pick.

Except that now it turned out that Jess didn't have the normal family that I'd thought. And it seemed that she was just as ashamed of her family as I was of mine. What a joke! There she was, with real parents and a sister, and yet she kept them all a massive secret. Why? Why was she so ashamed? I thought that her mother was nice. Sure, she was a hippy, but did that matter? At least she loved Jess, which is more than could be said for my mother. Either of my mothers, in fact. Nobody ever hugged me.

The water in the radiator was okay, so I hit the road again.

Maybe Jess wanted a different family. Maybe she didn't want her parents to break up and it'd been an ugly mess. Maybe they used to fight all the time, although I couldn't imagine her mother doing a lot of shouting. Maybe her sister's a drug addict and her father's on the dole. Maybe she had a different picture in her head about what her real family should be like. Just as I'd had, about her family.

When she didn't tell me about her background, I'd made it up. A fantasy story, really, with Jess as the fairy princess. And I was jealous, because I'd decided that her story was way better than mine. But of course, princesses don't go around dressed in jeans and a t-shirt, as Jess does, and anyway, since when have I believed in that fairy-tale bullshit?

But actually, in truth, I had. I'd thought everything would be so great once I'd found my real mother. I'd had such a clear picture of how it was going to be. Another fantasy. I was going to belong somewhere, with someone special. And I was going to discover that I was someone else, someone heaps better. I was going to get the chance to begin my life all over again. Rescued by a beautiful new mother who loved me and was always hugging me. Rescued from the evil parents who were not really my parents, who didn't love me, who wouldn't teach me to drive or let me watch what I wanted on TV. And then, suddenly, I found out that those ugly parents were blood relatives after all, and the beautiful new mother who was meant to rescue me turned out to be just old Aunty Lil. No wonder I'd crashed!

As for Jess, she wouldn't have had any expectations that she'd be rescued one day. She knew perfectly well that the family she had, was the one she'd be stuck with for the rest of her life. So perhaps that was why she hid the truth about her family. After all, it's only adopted kids like me who can dream of something better.

I arrived home, feeling totally wiped out and so decided to have a nap. I called Panadol, thinking that he'd want to join me, but he didn't show up. I whistled again, more loudly this time. Still nothing. I wandered through the house and the garden, but strangely I couldn't find him anywhere. It was only when I went down the side path and saw the open gate, that I realised what had happened.

I rushed into the street and looked up and down, but there was no sign of him. I then searched the whole neighbourhood, occasionally returning home to see if he'd made it back on his own. Around dinnertime, I discovered my parents in the kitchen but they couldn't remember if he'd been there when they'd gone out hours beforehand. Night fell. I kept looking, knowing how petrified poor little Panadol would be, out there in the dark and all alone.

The next day I combed the area once again and knocked on hundreds of doors, but nobody had seen him. So I took the week off work and continued to scour the streets. I rang the local vets and the ranger, plus I put notices up in most of the shop windows and stuck them onto light poles. I even put an ad in the local paper. However not one single person rang me with news.

Every evening I put his dinner out at the usual time and whistled, yet there was never the sound of running feet. In the morning the food in his bowl was always left untouched. My parents were convinced that he'd just turn up again but with each passing day, the nightmare dragged on, with no end in sight. It seemed as if Panadol had vanished off the face of the earth.

The ranger from the council suggested that it was worth checking the animal shelters so one day I drove to the largest one, the Stray

Dogs' Refuge. I walked into the office where a woman behind a counter was talking on the phone. I waited, nervously clutching Panadol's lead, and after a few minutes she hung up.

'I'm looking for my dog. He's sort of a Terrier, about this big,' I showed his height with my hand. 'He's white and tan. Is he here?'

'Was he wearing a collar?'

'Yes, a red one.'

'Any ID tag?'

'No.'

'Have a look out the back,' she said.

'Thanks, you've been a great help,' I muttered under my breath as I went out.

Although I'd heard barking when I was in the office, I wasn't prepared for the terrible noise that bombarded me the minute I opened the outside door. Every dog in the place seemed to be barking, or yapping, or howling, or yelping. It was deafening. I listened carefully for a minute, but couldn't make out Panadol's bark from the general racket.

I found myself standing next to a maze of corridors. I swung open a heavy metal gate into one of them and realised that it was totally covered in wire mesh. It was like a prison. I heard a thud and looked back. The gate had closed behind me.

On either side of the path there were yards. I looked into the first pen. There were seven big dogs just roaming around on the concrete floor. When they saw me, they rushed in a frenzied pack to the gate, barking hysterically. Some were pedigreed dogs, while others were crossbreeds. The smell of piss and dog turds and disinfectant just about made me puke, but I walked on. I had to find Panadol.

I looked into pen after pen. It seemed to take hours. There were yards for large male dogs and yards for large female dogs. Then there were all the yards for the smaller dogs, also divided up according to sex. There were special cages for puppies and individual ones for sick dogs.

Finally, there were no more pens left to inspect. I returned to the office.

'He's not here,' I said.

'Try again later.'

I nodded. 'By the way, you know the Labrador in the second yard on the right . . .'

'Number?'

'What?'

'What's the number of the tag on the dog?'

'I'm not sure. But I'm wondering why is Friday written on the gate to that pen? I think there's some day of the week on every gate.'

'That's when the dogs in that pen get assessed.'

'Oh. And what happens after that?'

'Some dogs are claimed by their owners before the time is up.'

'And what about the others?'

'Some are then moved into the adoption pens.'

'The what?'

'Where they're put up for sale.'

'But there's not many dogs in there. Where do the rest go?' I asked.

The woman just shrugged her shoulders and looked away.

'They surely don't get put down, do they?' I stammered.

'New dogs come in constantly.'

'You mean to say that you murder all those dogs?'

The woman just glared at me.

'But there are some beautiful ones out there – can't you even try to find them homes?'

At this, the woman became annoyed. 'Listen,' she snapped. 'You clearly have no idea of the scale of the problem. Over twenty thousand dogs are brought in to us every single year. We do our very best.'

'Why the hell should the dogs be put down when it's not their fault?'

'If you're such a crusader for dogs, why have you been so careless with your own?'

'It was my parents who—'

'It's always someone else's fault. Now, if you don't mind, I have work to do.'

I left immediately, slamming the door behind me.

A week later I went back to check if Panadol had at last made his way there. He hadn't. This time I also looked for the slobbering Labrador and the little white dog that shook like a leaf. I searched for the Kelpie cross, with the sad smile on her old grey face, and for the Dachshund who'd lost his bark. They were all gone. In fact, I hardly saw a dog I recognised. Over a hundred dogs – gone. A new lot of dogs, a different hundred dogs, frantically looked into my eyes and begged me to claim them. I walked through the mesh corridor, bawling. I didn't bother speaking to the woman in the office. I couldn't see any point.

There wasn't a day that went by when I didn't search for Panadol. Once I found a ginger cat, dead in the gutter. I picked it up in my jacket and knocked on lots of doors in that area before I finally located its owner. The elderly woman screamed when she first saw her cat, and then she burst into loud sobs. In a way, I felt jealous because at least she knew what had happened to her pet. I began hoping for some kind of a miracle.

Then one evening Daniel turned up at my place, with a large bunch of flowers.

'For Panadol,' he said. 'Nikki, I'm so very, very sorry.'

'Hey, I reckon that I'm still going to find him.'

However Daniel shook his head. And deep-down, I knew he was right. After he'd gone, I grabbed some old photos of Panadol but when I tried to look at them, I could barely see them through tears. I cried for hours and hours that night, because I knew that my beautiful little dog was lost to me forever. Finally I fell asleep, clutching those precious photos.

The next Saturday, I went back to the Stray Dogs' Refuge. I knew what I had to do. I looked in three pens and then in the fourth, I saw her – a black Labrador cross. She was standing quietly, with her nose pressed through the mesh. When the other dogs realised that

I was there, they rushed towards me, pushing her out of the way, as they barked and jumped at the gate. She lay down on the concrete floor and rested her head on her paws. She kept her sad, pleading eyes fixed on me, as if she knew that she was at the end of the road. 'Hey doggie,' I whispered. She wagged her tail gently at the sound of my voice.

Eventually, after the adoption papers had been signed, I was allowed to clip Panadol's old lead to her collar and remove her from the pack. She sped down the corridor with me in tow, past the other pens, past all the dogs who were headed to the death chamber. I couldn't look at them. They were barking frantically, desperately, and I wanted to block my ears against the noise. I had rescued one dog. It wasn't much, but it was all I could manage.

CLOSING DOORS
(Jess)

My mother stood in the doorway and asked, 'Was that Max on the phone?'

'No,' I lied.

'Then who were you talking to?'

I got off my bed and walked over to her.

'Kate, it's none of your business,' I said firmly, before I closed the door in her face.

But straight away the door was pushed open and she peered in. 'Are you okay? Is there anything you need?'

'Leave me alone! Please!'

'Are you hungry? Do you want me to make you a sandwich?'

I put my shoes on and ran as fast as I could out of the house. I didn't stop when I reached the road; I just kept on running. I went up a steep hill, then veered off down a narrow track through the bush and finally collapsed onto the ground. I was scarcely able to breathe, but at least I had escaped my mother and now had some privacy.

Why the hell had Max been shocked on the phone just now when I told him that we needed to break up? Hadn't he noticed that I'd been avoiding him? Obviously not. At the start of the phone call, he was so upset that I had actually felt sorry for him, but stopped when he launched into a spiel about how I had become a man-hater. In a very patronising voice, he assured me that this was completely understandable, given my near-rape experience. Apparently my negative reaction to men wouldn't last and then, according to him, I would naturally want to return to a relationship and, of course, to him.

'What an arrogant little shit!' I said aloud, so loudly that it startled a nearby mob of kangaroos into bounding away.

What gave Max the right to anoint himself as the expert on me and my life? And was he really that much of an idiot to believe that my decision to leave had nothing to do with him? He was wrong; in fact, it was entirely his fault. Over time, our relationship had become all about him. We always had to do whatever he wanted and go wherever he chose. There was never any negotiation, just the expectation that I would simply slot in with him. So what possible reason did I have to stay? I'd known for a while that I needed to leave and now that phone call absolutely confirmed it.

I stood up, wishing that I had a cigarette but unfortunately I had run out the previous evening. I considered heading back to the house, grabbing my wallet and driving the fifteen kilometres to the nearest shop. But I knew that my mother would be waiting for me at home, ready to pounce, and that she would insist on knowing where I was going and how long I would be out. If I told her that I was going to buy a packet of cigarettes, I'd cop a massive lecture about the dangers of smoking. Was it worth it? Not really, I decided.

I wandered back to the road, and watched a car go past. It was Liz, a neighbour, who waved cheerily. I sighed. What was I going to do now? Should I turn left or right? I opted to go left, away from the house, and I began scuffing my feet in the loose stones as I walked. Anything to delay having to put up with my mother and her incessant meddling.

Nikki couldn't keep her nose out of my business either.

'Where's Max?' she asked the instant I arrived at The Purple Crush, after a horrendous drive from the Bend.

'I don't know.'

'Have you broken up with him?'

'Yes.'

'Why?'

'I don't want a boyfriend at this point in my life. They're too much of a hassle.'

'Don't give me that feminist crap, Jess.'

'No, it's true. They stop us from getting on with our lives.'

'We're not talking about boyfriends, we're talking about Max. What wouldn't he let you do?'

I decided it was easier to change the subject. 'So what about playing some pool?' I asked.

'Won't the others be here any minute?'

'Come on. While we're waiting, we can have a couple of hits.'

'Nah. I'd rather talk.'

I managed to stifle a groan. 'What about?'

'I want to know how you're going.'

'I'm fine.'

'So you're okay?'

'Of course.'

'Then why aren't you back at class?'

'Too many other things to do. I'll return soon.'

'And what's it been like living with your mother again?'

Her question was exactly what I had dreaded. Now that Nikki had forced her way through the door into my private life and had taken a good look around, it was proving difficult to close the door again. I decided on subterfuge.

'Wonderful. It's great to have all my meals provided.'

'Is this why you haven't moved back to your flat?'

I've never been so grateful to see Daniel and Amanda as I was then.

'Sorry we're late,' said Amanda. 'We got stuck in football traffic.'

The coin toss decided that Nikki and I would play against Daniel and Amanda. As I chalked my cue, I looked sideways at Nikki, interested to see how she was faring these days with Amanda and was astonished to discover that all animosity seemed to have disappeared.

I was also surprised to see how well Daniel and Amanda played together. By the time it was my shot, they had sunk four balls, to our two. I took careful aim and headed the ball towards the pocket. I surveyed the rest of the table to decide which to play next.

'Oh, bad luck,' murmured Amanda.

I refocussed and realised that the ball was still there. It hadn't dropped into the pocket. I had missed. Nikki was staring at me, open-mouthed. I shrugged my shoulders, passed Daniel the cue and sat down.

That had been an easy shot. Anybody could see that. So why hadn't the ball gone in? Was I losing my touch?

The game turned into a complete disaster. I watched Amanda and Daniel sink ball after ball. Nikki did fairly well, but I couldn't seem to get them in, not even those in a straight line to a pocket. The game was over in an incredibly short period of time. Amanda potted the black with a resounding whack. I had lost.

'It's just an off-day for you, Jess,' said Daniel. 'Perhaps you're out of practice?'

There was silence while they all waited for me to reply, yet I had absolutely no idea what to say. I always won.

'What about a rematch?' asked Amanda. 'Maybe you'll return to your usual form.'

I shook my head, unable to speak.

'Hey,' Nikki interrupted. 'Does everyone know about Lucky?'

'Who?' asked Amanda.

'Lucky is my new dog. She's a Labrador cross.'

Why was Nikki so keen, all of a sudden, to commandeer the conversation? Was it because she knew that she was within striking distance of winning against me and that she could sense how weak I had become?

'So tell me, how's your car going?' I asked, although I already knew the answer. 'Did you have many problems fixing it?'

Nikki's face fell.

'A few.'

'What's wrong with The Beast? Why doesn't anybody tell me anything anymore?' whined Daniel.

I watched Nikki and Amanda exchange a quick glance. Had they privately discussed Daniel? Were they now collaborators instead of rivals?

'Don't worry, The Beast is fully mobile again,' Nikki told Daniel. 'Anyway, back to Lucky. I rescued her from the Stray Dogs' Refuge, although why it's called a "refuge" I'll never know. Most of the dogs in there end up getting murdered and I'm pretty sure that they get massacred all together.'

Nikki was sometimes so melodramatic that she made me want to laugh. Fortunately I didn't, because Daniel was clearly shocked.

'That's terrible! How many dogs are in there?'

'Over a hundred. And all kinds, even pedigree dogs. And I'm only talking about one place; there are others.'

'Surely though, the dogs have become accidentally lost and their owners come to claim them?'

'I saw some getting out, but not many. I also saw dogs being brought in, by people who didn't want their pet anymore.'

'How come? Were they vicious?' asked Amanda.

'Vicious?' Nikki snorted. 'One family turned up with their Cocker Spaniel. They didn't want him because they'd decided he was too old to run in the park with the kids. That poor little dog was absolutely petrified, and had to be dragged across the floor by the collar before being taken outside. The family picked out a new puppy. Since it's the young dogs who are put up for adoption, that old Cocker would've been murdered straight away.'

'That's appalling,' Daniel cried.

'Sure is.' Nikki paused for a minute, finished her Coke and then added, 'One time I watched a guy bring in his Bull Terrier because the dog was deaf.'

I couldn't contain myself any longer. 'Do you think he should have been fitted with hearing aids?' I grinned.

They all glared at me.

'It's only a dog,' I reminded them. I mean, where was their sense of proportion?

'Only a dog? Does that mean that he's got no right to live if he's deaf? You think he should be killed?'

'Dogs are considered to be man's best friend,' Daniel intercepted quickly. 'How can man discard his best friend so easily?'

'Because we live in a throw-away world. What we don't want anymore, we chuck away. Whether it's a pizza box or a poor little dog.' Nikki slumped down into her chair.

'Yes, consumerism is fundamental to a capitalist society,' I agreed aloud, but added silently, 'and lots more things are thrown onto the rubbish heap than dogs.'

Daniel shook his head forlornly. 'Gandhi said you can tell what sort of society it is by the way it treats its animals,' he muttered. 'Anyway, Nik, how long do I have to wait before I have the honour of meeting Ms Lucky?'

'Nikki hasn't mentioned to you that Lucky is a radical lesbian separatist, who refuses to mix with men?' I quipped and stood up. 'Who wants another drink?'

Amanda jumped to her feet as well and we took the others' orders. I waited until we were out of earshot before speaking.

'I can't believe it! We've just spent all that time discussing dogs. Dogs!'

'Ridiculous!' agreed Amanda. 'Everyone knows that cats are far superior.'

I stared at her for a full minute. 'Cats or dogs,' I finally said, 'both carry the same type of fleas.'

I marched off to the toilets, leaving her to carry the drinks back to the table. When I returned, the topic had changed. However, my relief was short-lived.

'I wish,' I heard Nikki say as I sat back down, 'that I had a totally different family to the one I've got.' She sighed, before adding, 'You feel the same way, don't you, Jess? And yours is a real family.'

I froze, my coffee suspended mid-air. Thankfully, the discussion headed off in another direction.

'What do you mean?' Daniel asked. 'What's a "real" family?'

'One that has two parents who are biologically related to the kids.'

'Whoa. Let me get this straight. You're saying that real parents are your biological parents and not your adopted parents?'

'Of course.'

'So it's the genetic link that makes them the real deal?' asked Amanda.

'Yeah.'

'But isn't your adopting mother part of the same gene pool as you?'

'Well, I guess, but . . . she wasn't the one who gave birth to me.'

'I don't know much about genetics or birth-related stuff,' Daniel said, 'but isn't your real mother the one who takes care of you?'

'Are you stupid or what?'

Why does Nikki always think that the other person doesn't understand, when actually they're just seeing things from a different perspective? Daniel, in fact, had made a valid point.

'No,' Nikki continued on, regardless. 'My real mother gave birth to me and then immediately chucked me away.'

'But why do you reckon that she's your real mother if this is what she did?' asked Daniel, very sensibly.

Nikki didn't know how to reply to this and so there was a slight pause. Then Amanda said,

'Your poor mother. It must've been so hard to give up her newborn baby.'

'You've got to be joking!' exploded Nikki. 'She couldn't have cared less!'

'I find that impossible to believe.'

'The only person who ever goddamn suffered as a result of my birth was me.'

We all stared at Nikki. She was so intractably bitter that she discounted that her mother could also have feelings. It wasn't right. Suddenly I thought of a way to get Nikki to see reason.

'How did you feel when you lost Panadol?' I asked.

The question threw her for a minute.

'Pretty bad,' she finally managed.

'Did you miss him?'

'Of course.'

I could see her fighting back the tears.

'Because he was your dog and you loved him?'

She nodded.

'So how do you think Lil felt when she no longer had you?'

'What?'

'Surely Lil would have been devastated about losing her baby, just like you were when you lost your dog.'

'Absolute bullshit. Lil chose to get rid of me!'

'But the decision wouldn't have been easy for her, Nikki.'

'How would you bloody know? Since when did you become the world's leading authority on mothers?'

I said nothing, sensing danger. I was aware that she had the ammunition.

'How come,' she continued, 'you know so much about my mother when you don't have much of a clue about your own?'

What the hell did she mean by that? I was certainly not about to ask her.

'Stop it, you two!' Amanda intervened. 'We're all on the same side.'

Are we? After Nikki's nasty outburst, I really didn't think so.

To my surprise, Nikki sighed.

'I'm sorry, Jess.'

'I am too,' I said, although frankly, I had no idea why I was apologising.

'I guess,' Nikki went on, 'that I was feeling a bit defensive, so I launched into attack mode.'

I stared at her. She was right. That was exactly what she had done. Maybe she was making progress, after all.

'So can we get back to our discussion?' asked Daniel. 'Nikki, can you explain to us what exactly constitutes this so-called "real" family?'

'Two parents who are your biological parents, and at least one brother or sister.'

We all looked at Nikki in astonishment, again.

'And what about grandparents, aunts, uncles and cousins?' asked Amanda.

'I'm talking about the family you live with, not the whole goddamn family tree!'

'Hey! I happen to live with my grandparents, my parents, my sisters, an uncle and two cousins. Does this mean that this isn't a real family?'

I smiled to myself. How was Nikki going to fit Amanda's Vietnamese extended family into her ridiculously narrow definition?

'I'm referring to Australian families.'

'I'm Australian. I was born here.'

'But your parents weren't.'

Before Amanda could reply, I interrupted.

'You're referring to a nuclear family, Nikki.'

'Maybe.'

'Anyway, in today's society, high divorce rates have resulted in many single-parent households and if the parents marry again, blended families. Then these days there's IVF, donor sperm and surrogacy which also mess with your theory. And lots of families have only one child, for a multitude of reasons. Plus, as Amanda points out, there are extended families. Have I forgotten to include anything?'

'I doubt it,' said a voice to my left. It was Max. What was he doing here? I hadn't invited him. He grabbed a chair from another table and sat down next to Daniel.

'Anyway,' I went on, 'all of these factors challenge the stereotype of a traditional nuclear family.'

'Hmm. So who has one of these conventional families?' asked Daniel.

'Not me,' said Nikki, 'because I'm adopted and not Jess, because hers doesn't fit either. Amanda's family doesn't count because it's Vietnamese.'

'That's not fair.'

'But it is different, isn't it?'

'I guess that we have our own cultural norms,' muttered Amanda.

'There must be a goddamn normal family out there somewhere,' insisted Nikki. 'What about yours, Daniel? It seems pretty standard to me.'

'Very funny.'

'You've got two parents and a sister. That's nice and ordinary.'

'No, it's not.'

'How come?'

'It just isn't!'

'Come on, Daniel, there's nothing to be ashamed about having a family that fits the stereotype,' I laughed.

'No!' he suddenly shouted. 'I am NOT ashamed! It's fine by me that my sister is gay and I thought it was great when she finally came out of the closet. But since then, there's been a massive rift in my family. My parents belong to an ultra-conservative church which believes that lesbianism is a cardinal sin, and so they're refusing to acknowledge that my sister is gay. It's a complete and utter mess.'

Not one of us knew how to respond, so there was silence. Max was the first to speak.

'Mate, your family was never in the running to be considered typical, anyway. You lot don't eat meat! You're bloody vegetarians!' He gently slapped Daniel on the shoulder.

'So do we know of any actual family that fits the stereotype?' I asked.

'No, not a single one!' Max said. 'For the simple reason that they actually don't exist, outside of movies and television. They're a myth.'

I stared at him. He was 100% right. I had always understood that there was no such thing as a normal family, and yet I had continually measured my own family against the myth, rating it two out of ten. An abject failure in an absurd exam. What an idiot I'd been.

Meanwhile Daniel was saying, 'I've always wished that I belonged to someone else's family.'

'Me too,' nodded Amanda. 'And do you ever look around the room at family gatherings and wonder who on earth these people are?'

'Constantly.'

I knew exactly what Daniel and Amanda meant.

'So none of us feel like we fit,' said Nikki slowly. 'We've all been sucked in by the bullshit. Maybe it's time to put this silly dream aside and accept that we're stuck with the families we've already got.'

'Yes, but I don't think that we have to accept everything,' put in Amanda. 'We've still got choices. For example, I was given a name by my parents which I disliked, and so I changed it. Simple!'

'What was it?'

'Huong.'

'But why change it? Are you embarrassed about being Vietnamese?' asked Daniel.

'Not exactly. It's just that I feel more Australian than Vietnamese.'

'Why do you have to be one or the other?'

'Actually I'm Huong at home and in my community, and Amanda everywhere else.'

Hmm. So she didn't really change it; she just added a second, different name. Did that mean that I could be both Karma and Jess, depending on the context?

'Can we head off now?' Daniel asked, interrupting my thoughts.

I glanced at Nikki to check her reaction but it wasn't Amanda who got to her feet, but Max.

'See you 'round.'

The two guys strolled off together.

Amanda and Nikki both turned to me.

'Are you okay, Jess?' asked Nikki.

'Why wouldn't I be?'

And to be perfectly honest, I was glad to see the back of him. I didn't need Max, or any boyfriend, for that matter. I was much better off on my own.

I gave Nikki the same advice when she rang two days later.

'Don't waste your time worrying about guys,' I told her. 'They're not worth it. Get on with your own life.'

'But do you think I like Daniel?' she asked again, almost yelling over the background noise of the garage. 'What do you reckon?'

I sighed to myself. She clearly wasn't going to let up. 'Of course you do.'

'Not just as a friend.'

'I know what you mean, and my answer is still yes.'

'What should I do?'

'Nothing,' I said, before adding, 'besides, you know Daniel isn't interested in you.'

Nikki muttered that she had to get back to work and hung up. But ten minutes later, the phone rang again.

'Jess, I've been thinking. I don't want to play pool with you anymore.'

'You've already told me that.'

'Yes, but I really mean it now.'

'So do you think that I'm no longer worth beating?'

'Don't be stupid.'

'Well then, why?'

'It's kind of hard to explain.'

'I hope that you're not feeling sorry for me because I lost the other day.'

'Why would I bother doing that? You were just having an off-day.'

'I played incredibly badly, didn't I.'

'Big deal. Even international champions can stuff up once in a while.'

'So why have you banned our games of pool? Are you still tired of always losing, as you told me a while ago?'

'Don't get me wrong, Jess. I'd much rather win than lose. But not if winning means beating you.'

I heard the phone being picked up on another extension. 'Kate!' I shouted. 'I'm already here! Get off the line!' I waited until she had hung up.

'Sorry, Nikki. What were you saying?'

'I don't want you to lose and me to win.'

'I don't get it.'

'You're not the competition, Jess. I've realised that.'

'So who is?'

'Dunno, but I know it isn't you.'

'Oh.'

'I'd better go. Have to get back to doing a service on a Commodore. See you.'

I hung up the phone slowly. She had changed. This was a Nikki I didn't know, and certainly didn't understand. I was still trying to get a handle on this new Nikki, when my mother walked in.

'How's Max?' she asked. 'When are we going to meet him?'

'Kate! Leave me alone!' I raced out of the room, slamming the door behind me.

INTO TOP GEAR
(Nikki)

Exactly as Fred had shown me, I went very slowly and carefully over the whole surface of the Corolla with a magnet. The brand-new duco was high gloss but I knew that rust could be lurking below the shiny exterior. Fred was checking out the car for his nephew and I'd been given the job of rust detector.

'Hey, Fred,' I called. 'There's a lot of bog here.'

He crawled out from underneath the chassis, looked at where I was pointing and told me to write it all down on a piece of paper.

After half an hour, I'd drawn a diagram of the car with five different places that had been filled with bog. Obviously it had been in multiple bingles and although it had been repaired, everyone knows that this doesn't stop the spread of rust. When I told Fred that the car wasn't worth buying, he grinned and slapped me on the back. I'd done a good job!

I began a major service on a Commodore, thinking that if I hadn't done the magnet trick then I wouldn't have realised what a rust-bucket the Corolla was. I would've been completely sucked in by what it looked like on the outside. I wasn't a loser, after all. I could fix cars, so long as I knew what to look for and didn't get taken in by the crap.

I downed tools, wiped my hands on a rag and went into the office to ring Daniel to let him know about the magnet trick. But it was his mother who answered the phone, and when she told me that he'd left early for class, I felt a strange stab of disappointment.

I grabbed the office chair and quickly sat down. Had Amanda understood more about the way I felt than I had myself? Could it be true that I really did like Daniel? All of a sudden, I realised that in fact, I did.

Panicking, I dialled Jess's number. She's had much more experience than I have with this kind of stuff so naturally I expected that she would know what to do. Ha! She just launched into a tirade about how we didn't need boyfriends and how they were a complete waste of time! This really pissed me off as she's the one who always has a boyfriend, while I never do.

However Jess was right about one thing – I happened to like a guy who didn't like me. Daniel was chasing after Amanda, and even though she'd told me that she wasn't interested in him, this certainly didn't mean that he was ever going to notice me.

I sighed and went back to work on the Commodore, wondering why I kept hitting my head against a brick wall even when I knew that I was going to come off second best. All my life I'd felt like such a loser and yet I kept putting myself into situations where it was obvious that I was going to fail. Like playing pool against Jess. She always won when it was just us two, which meant that I always lost. I was so tired of being beaten, and had felt this way for ages, but now something else dawned on me as well. I realised that I no longer wanted to beat my friend. What would be the point of Jess becoming the loser instead of me, and for me to be the winner instead of her? No. I was sick to death of the competition between us. It was a game that I no longer wanted to play, and it was time for it to end.

I rang Jess back and told her, but she didn't have a clue what I was talking about. It made me wonder why it was so important to her that she kept playing against me, and beating me. Was there something she was trying to prove? Did this mean that she didn't feel much like a winner either?

And what was going on for her at the moment? Had she dropped out of her course? And why hadn't she moved back to her flat? Jess kept insisting that she was okay but frankly, I had my doubts.

Suddenly I had an idea. I'd buy her a pool cue. I thought back to when I'd first got my job as an apprentice and she'd bought me a spanner. While I hadn't appreciated it at the time, that spanner was a great present and still held prime real estate on my bedroom wall. Maybe the pool cue would help Jess deal with whatever was going on for her at the moment. Yes! I decided that this was an excellent plan. I was definitely on a roll.

Not so, however, with Lucky. What the hell was I going to do about her? She was constantly pulling washing off the line, digging up the garden and barking, and with her, I had no plan. Clearly I needed help and so one Saturday morning I rang a radio show to talk to Dr Hugh, a vet. But to my surprise, he acted like it was all my fault.

'Don't you realise that she's BORED?' he shouted. 'You have to get a second dog!'

'But I don't want another one.'

Well, that was a mistake. He became even angrier.

'It's not about what you want, it's about what your poor dog needs! And you MUST walk her three times a day!'

'How can I do that when I work?'

'Get someone else to take her out! Your parents, a neighbour, an unemployed teenager – ANYONE! That dog needs more attention and more exercise!'

I tried to explain that my parents didn't like Lucky and that they certainly weren't going to take her for a walk, but he wouldn't listen.

'You got the dog! It's your responsibility to look after her!' he said, before we were disconnected.

I looked outside to find that Lucky had trashed the flyscreen door. I tried to stick the wire back on so that my parents wouldn't notice, but it wouldn't hold. Instead I decided to take her out on a lead. Maybe Dr Hugh was right; she did need more exercise.

But half way around the block, my arm was killing me. Lucky pulled all the time and I could only just stop her from rushing up to every cat, kid, car, piece of rubbish, tree, gate, other dog or person she saw. I gave up, turned around and put her back in the yard. I went inside, exhausted, and while I had a cup of coffee, I watched her begin to shred the doormat. I sighed. I'd made such a mistake in getting her. No wonder she'd been in the dog shelter – she was way out of control. And she wasn't even grateful to me for rescuing her!

Half an hour later, my parents returned home. Lil was with them. The three of them took one look at the devastation and all began yelling simultaneously.

'The door is ruined!' screamed my father.

'That doormat was new!' my mother shouted.

'Oh my goodness! Enough is enough!' Lil cried.

My father pointed to Lucky, who was by this stage lying on the remains of the doormat, panting.

'Nikki,' he ordered, 'that dog has to go!'

I glared at him and shook my head.

'Just look at the damage that he's done!'

'I've told you a million times that Lucky is female! Why can't you remember this?'

'You have to take the dog back to wherever you got him from. Today.'

'I won't.'

'You don't have any choice.'

'She's my dog. You can't make that decision.'

'This is my house and while you're under this roof, you have to do what I tell you.'

'You really must get rid of it,' said Lil.

I turned to face her. 'Ah yes, the perfect solution. Just chuck her away. You know all about that, don't you, Lily. It doesn't matter how she feels about it.'

'Don't be ridiculous, Nikki. It doesn't feel anything. It's a dog!'

'And a terrible dog, in actual fact,' chimed in my father. 'What on earth made you adopt him?'

'So you think she has defective genes? She comes from bad genetic stock?'

'I don't care where the dog comes from, so long as he goes back!'

My mother suddenly struggled to her feet.

'Sit down, Ivy!' ordered Lil.

She collapsed back into her chair.

'Nikki, take the dog now and don't return until you've disposed of him,' my father said.

'Immediately,' agreed Lil.

I looked from one to the other, and then I looked at Lucky. I realised that she needed me to save her. Again.

'NO! Lucky is staying here. This is her home now and she's mine.' I started to cry.

My mother stood up again. 'In my opinion,' she said quietly, 'Nikki should be allowed to keep the dog.'

'Stay out of it, Ivy,' snapped Lil.

'Sit down,' ordered my father.

But she didn't. Instead, she continued on. 'Nikki is right. The dog belongs with her.'

My father and Lil both stared at her, and there was a strange silence.

'The dog is hers and is staying,' she insisted. 'End of discussion.'

Nobody looked at me.

'Now, would anyone like a cup of tea?' my mother asked calmly.

She left the room and we heard her fill the kettle.

I wiped my face with my sleeve, completely dumbfounded. My mother had actually stood up for me! Never before had she done this. I didn't know what to do. And then, suddenly, I realised something. This woman was the only mother I'd ever had. She was the one who'd always been there for me. She had made my school lunch every single day and she had rushed me to hospital when I'd fallen out of a tree. I remembered the time that I'd accidently broken the antique vase in the hallway, and she'd glued it back together again so that my father was none the wiser. To be sure, she was never going to win an award for being the greatest mother in the world, but she was my mother.

Right at this moment, Lucky barked. I looked across at her and understood what I had to do. I grabbed my car keys, drove to the local pet shop and bought a brand-new kennel, because Panadol's was in actual fact way too small. I chose a bone that would keep her busy for days and after talking to the shop assistant, I bought a new kind of walking apparatus. Dr Hugh was right, after all. Lucky needed to be taken out and shown the neighbourhood. It wasn't her fault that she was so naughty. She'd had a terrible start in life and anyway, she was just behaving like a dog. It was up to me to train her and look after her the best I could, because she was my responsibility and because I loved her.

A week later, I ran into Daniel and told him my big news.

'Hey! I've taught Lucky how to go on a lead, without pulling! And she now sits on command.'

'That's good.'

'Could I please have a bit more enthusiasm? It's been incredibly hard to get her to do these things.'

'Congratulations.'

'Seriously? That's the best you can do?'

To my surprise, Daniel instead said, 'You're looking very nice today, Nikki.'

'Okay, cut the crap and tell me what you want to borrow.'

'Huh?'

'It'd better not be my timing light. I've told you before that it's off the free trade list. You know how important it is to me. I don't ask to borrow your feeler gauges.'

'Listen,' he snapped, 'I was paying you a compliment.'

'How come when I was wearing these exact same overalls last week, you didn't mention how gorgeous I looked then?'

'What sort of girl are you that you don't appreciate a compliment?'

'Hmm. Perhaps I'm not a girl. Hang on a minute.' I patted my chest. 'Yes, we have confirmation,' I laughed. That did the trick. Daniel grinned and whatever weird mood he'd been in, seemed to pass.

'Do you fancy getting something to eat?'

'Of course,' I said, beginning to walk towards the caf.

'Nah, let's go somewhere different. What about going to that grotty place round the corner for a change? I'll show you the new colour of my car on the way.'

We changed direction.

'You mean that you've finally got around to respraying it? Miracles do happen, after all. What colour did you end up with?'

'Midnight blue. It looks great, even if I say so myself.'

'So when are you going to do my car?'

'In your dreams!'

We arrived at his car and I admired the new paint work. He'd done a reasonable job, although it was a bit patchy on the passenger-side door. However I decided not to mention this, especially after the strange way he'd been acting.

We ordered our meals the minute we sat down in the cafe. I was starving, and so began demolishing the bread. Daniel was fiddling with everything within reach on the table. There was obviously something wrong.

'What's up?' I asked.

'I was just wondering . . .' he hesitated before continuing, 'are you doing anything tomorrow night?'

'Why?'

'I thought that maybe . . .'

I waited.

'Do you want to go out with me?' he rushed.

'What? Just you and me?'

He nodded.

'On a date?'

'Well, yes.'

I stared at him, shocked. I leapt to my feet, accidentally knocking over my chair.

'I can't believe what you just suggested!'

'Forget it,' Daniel whispered, looking around the restaurant.

'What about Amanda?' I shouted.

'Amanda? What's she got to do with any of this?'

'Excuse me,' a voice behind me said, 'is this boy making a nuisance of himself?'

I turned around to find the waitress, and then I realised that everyone in the whole place was gawking.

'I'm sorry, Nikki. I didn't mean to . . .' Red in the face, Daniel jumped up and flew out the door.

'Well, that got rid of him, didn't it,' grinned the waitress. 'Two-timing bastard!'

It took me a minute to understand what she had said. 'No,' I cried and ran out after him. I quickly caught up.

'That was quite a performance you put on back there,' Daniel muttered.

'You should've given me some warning. You took me completely by surprise.'

'This is all my fault?' he snapped and walked faster.

'Okay, okay. I guess that I went a bit over the top, didn't I? I just wasn't expecting it.'

'A bit?'

'All right, a lot. But I am sorry.'

And I was. Daniel was extremely angry with me – I'd never seen him so angry – and I had no idea how I was going to undo what had just happened. We arrived back at his car and I desperately wished that he wouldn't get in. He did, but at least he wound the window down.

'Well, be seeing you.'

I said nothing. I didn't want to give him the green light to drive off.

He switched on the ignition.

'Hey,' I said, reaching inside the car to pat him on his shoulder, 'I really do like the new paint job.' I felt I had to say something.

His whole expression changed, and when I looked down, I realised that I'd forgotten to take my hand off his shoulder. I felt an electric current zap through my body, and wondered if he'd felt it too. I quickly took my hand away. He turned off the car, got out and walked around to the back.

'Sit down, Nik,' he ordered, opening the boot.

I parked myself in the boot and he took a seat beside me.

'I don't want to wreck our friendship over all of this,' he said.

'Neither do I.'

He seemed to relax a little. 'You and I are mates, above all else, aren't we?'

'Of course.' I grinned, to hide my lie.

'So why did you carry on like that when all I asked was if you'd go out with me?'

All? I thought, looking into his beautiful brown eyes. I suddenly realised that by stacking on such a scene, I'd run the risk of showing him how I really felt. I had to be careful. Daniel was not stupid.

'Why?' he asked again, his eyes not leaving my face.

I stalled for time.

'Yeah, I know. I shouldn't have chucked such a massive wobbly,' I sighed. 'I mean, it's not like you want to go to bed with me or anything.'

To my total amazement, I watched his eyes slide guiltily away from mine. He laughed, just a little too loudly. I stared at him; I couldn't help it. For in that moment, I realised that he did in fact want to go to bed with me. His face had turned a deep shade of red, and he was studying his knees. I took a deep breath. Although his feelings had been exposed by accident, I owed him some honesty too. It was only fair.

'Daniel,' I began, but it was hard to know what to say. 'I don't understand why . . . How come you . . .' Finally, I decided to go straight to the point. 'I thought that you liked Amanda.'

It was his turn to stall.

'No, not really. Well, maybe. But only for a short while.'

'You were totally gaga over her. I saw you.'

'That's not true.'

Why was he denying it? I wondered. I decided to change lanes.

'Anyway, I needed you to help me with The Beast after I'd had the accident and you were too busy running after her to waste your time with me.'

'But you didn't let me know what was happening. I didn't realise that you needed help.'

'You weren't around long enough for me to tell you anything.'

'I'm sorry.'

'I felt so jealous of Amanda.'

'Why?'

'Because you were drooling over her and not me.'

'But you were my friend, Nik.'

'I know that. But why didn't you notice me?'

'I just didn't see you in that way.'

'Why not?' I wailed, and hoped that he wouldn't mention the fact that she was a babe, while I wasn't.

'Nik, I guess that I saw you as my mate and not as potential girlfriend material. I don't have any other explanation.'

I looked at Daniel and sighed. I knew that it wasn't his fault. It just was. And after all, I myself hadn't been interested in him until recently. I'd seen him as my mate, and had checked out other guys as possible boyfriends. Like that arsehole Gary, I'm ashamed to say. Spunky guys I didn't actually know, so that I could make up a total fantasy story about who they were and how we could be together. They weren't real.

Daniel was grinning at me. 'If it's any consolation, Amanda's now my mate, and it's you I want as a girlfriend.'

'But I don't see that it's got to be one or the other. After all, I still want to be your mate,' I said.

He winked at me. 'But you'd also like a bit of drooling as well?'

'Maybe a bit.'

'I can only manage drooling if you lend me the timing light for the duration,' he said.

I laughed then. He could have my body any day of the week, but never my timing light. Daniel must have read my thoughts, well, half of them at any rate, for he reached across for me. He pulled me in close and I put my arms around him. We sat there for ages, snuggled up together in the boot of his car. I have to confess that it did feel really weird, after all that time being friends, but it also felt bloody fantastic!

SOME SURPRISES
(Jess)

I heard someone yell, 'Are you there, Karma?'

Walking into the kitchen, I found Liz opening the pantry door. 'I need some baking powder for Matt's birthday cake,' she explained as she searched. 'Fourteen today – can you believe it?'

'Really? I remember holding him when he was just a baby.'

'I know. It doesn't seem all that long ago,' Liz sighed, finding what she wanted and putting the little container down on the bench. 'Anyway, how's things? Your mother is quite worried about you.'

'I'm fine.'

'Are you back at TAFE?'

'Kind of.'

'And how's it going with Max?'

'We broke up.'

'Oh Jess, I am sorry. Another failed relationship. Never mind, you've still got plenty of time to find the right one.'

'Hmm. Like you did, Liz?' I asked, raising my eyebrows at her.

'Touché! I know that my Mr Right left for a younger woman, but at least by then I had the two boys.'

'I'm not sure that I want kids.'

'What? Of course you do! Every woman wants to be a mother. It's only natural. Okay, maybe you don't feel that strongly about it now as you're only twenty-one, but I'm sure that later on, when your biological clock starts ticking, it'll be a whole other story.'

'My watch happens to be digital and so is my alarm clock. No ticking!'

Liz laughed, before looking at her own watch. 'Standing here chatting isn't going to get that cake into the oven. If you're around this afternoon, come over for a piece and wish Matt a happy birthday.

He'd like that.' She gave me a hug, grabbed the baking powder and rushed out the door.

I made a cup of coffee while I mulled over our conversation. Why the hell does Liz assume that I want kids and that it's inevitable that I'll have some? And why does everyone make the same assumption? Surely it's a choice, and one that is up to me to make? Yet Liz believes that my biology is going to take over and make this extremely important decision for me. As a woman, apparently, my life has already been predetermined and I don't get to choose. Seriously? Is this really how it is, and how it should be?

I took another gulp of coffee. Yes, of course I understand that it's part of the natural order to reproduce – we are animals, after all – but haven't I already been circumventing the natural order by choosing to use contraception when I have sex? So wouldn't I have to make a decision to stop doing this?

I drained the last of my coffee and took the cup back into the kitchen, where the clock on the wall informed me that I was late, so I had to run all the way over to Jane's house. Jane had promised to lend me something to wear for a party that night, but when I viewed the items of clothing she had already laid out on her bed, I immediately shook my head.

'You're joking, right? Dresses? For me?' She knows that I never wear dresses.

'Not unusual attire for women, especially to more formal occasions,' Jane said, clearly mocking me.

'Hmph. Got any pants that might fit?'

'Let me see.'

'You do realise that women fought long and hard for the right to wear pants, don't you?'

'And you're telling me that it's your job to keep the revolution alive?'

I sighed. 'It's just that I prefer to wear pants. I feel more comfortable in them. Besides, I've got spindly legs.'

'That's not true.'

'How do you know? Have you ever seen them?'

'You're impossible! Now what about these?'

Jane had pulled out a pair of plain, black pants.

'Perfect,' I said. 'Can I try them on? And by any chance, do you have some sort of top to go with them? Doesn't have to be anything fancy. And maybe a jacket?'

When I left, I was carrying a whole outfit under my arm. I was all set – the only thing that I now had to do was to change my attitude about going. It was Melissa's twenty-first birthday party and I'd been surprised to receive my invitation in the mail, for while we'd been good friends at school, we'd hardly kept in touch since. At any rate, I felt obliged to go, and was dreading it.

The minute I arrived at the party, I scanned the room for the three other friends who'd been part of our circle at school and was devastated to see none of them. However the birthday girl rushed up to me.

'So glad that you could make it, Karma!' Melissa gushed. 'How are you? Did you have any trouble finding the place?'

'It's Jess now,' I said, but she wasn't listening. She grabbed my arm and steered me across the room, coming to a stop in front of her brother.

'Do you remember Tom?' she asked, before racing away.

Of course I remembered him – how could I not? We had clashed numerous times over politics. I smiled politely, but he merely scowled in return.

'So are you still the little radical that you once were, or have you finally grown up?'

'Oh. And have you remained a right-wing conservative who has no respect for women?'

We glared at each other. I turned around to see who else I could talk to but there was no-one. I looked back at Tom.

'Did you finish your engineering degree?'

'Of course.'

'And are you working now as an engineer?'

'Yes.'

'How do you like it?'

'It's okay.'

There was an awkward pause.

'Are you married?' he asked.

'No.'

'Why not? Nobody wants you? Well, that's to be expected!' he sneered nastily.

'What?' I stammered.

He clearly wasn't with anyone either, and yet he was having a go at me? I went to storm off, but in that split second, I thought of Nikki and changed my mind.

'Tom,' I said, looking him full in the face, 'you're an absolute ARSEHOLE!'

Calmly, I walked away, to stand on my own in that crowded, noisy room. Everyone was in pairs or in groups, but I didn't care. Being alone was far preferable to being stuck with Tom. I amused myself by watching several people talking animatedly together as part of a large group, when a very overweight guy noticed me and lumbered over.

'Howdy, little lady. All on your lonesome? Do you need to be rescued?' he asked.

'No,' I replied. 'I don't.' He looked so crestfallen that I added more kindly, 'But thanks anyway.'

He remained where he was, opposite me. Now what was I going to do?

'Er, do you spend a lot of time watching old cowboy movies?' I asked, to break the awkward silence.

'Wow! How the heck did you figure that out?'

The idiot just stood there, grinning at me.

'You're here!' someone yelled over my shoulder. 'Thank God!'

I swivelled around and was overjoyed to find my old school mate Julie. I hugged her, before grabbing her by the hand and leading her away.

'Thanks for saving me!' I said, once we were out of earshot. 'Being a woman on her own at a party is not a whole lot of fun. I'd forgotten.'

Julie nodded. 'Trust me, I know. So where's Luke?'

'Long gone. The latest was Max. Hey, there aren't any chairs.'

I was glad that I'd worn pants when I saw how difficult it was for Julie in her mini-skirt to sit on the floor. Eventually she took off her jacket, draped it over her lap and was then visibly more at ease. With our backs resting up against a wall, we talked for hours; we had a lot of catching up to do.

It was therefore very late by the time we said goodbye and I left the party. As I walked along the deserted streets through the drizzling rain, I realised that I hadn't been out at night since that terrible episode at TAFE. I strode along, turning every now and then, just to make sure that nobody was behind me, and finally arrived at the multi-storey car park.

But as I went to enter, I found a thickset middle-aged man standing in the middle of the roadway, blocking my path. What the hell was he doing there? Was he waiting for me? I stopped dead in my tracks but I knew that to get to my car, I had to pass him. There was no other option. I took a deep breath and marched, head down, towards him.

'Hi,' he said. 'Have you had a good night?'

I could feel him staring at me but I didn't look up as I walked steadily past him. Reaching the stairwell, I ran up two steps at a time and raced across the empty expanse of car park. I made it to my car, the only one left, and desperately fished for my keys in my backpack. Where were they? I found them, opened the door and jumped in. Straight away I locked all the doors, and it was only then that I allowed myself to check if he had followed me. Nobody was there. I slumped over the steering wheel, feeling relief wash over me, as I gasped for breath.

My hands were trembling. Who was that man? Did he have a knife? What did he want? Why had I become such a target? Suddenly

I realised that he could turn up again at any moment and there I was, stuck in the car. I had to get out of there, immediately.

I sped around the car park and quickly arrived at the exit. There, in the little booth, was the same man I had just seen. Was I going to have to talk to him now? The boom was down and I couldn't go forward. I was trapped.

'Have you got your ticket?'

Was he the parking attendant?

I wound down the window, but only enough to be able to hand my ticket through the slit.

'That'll be twenty dollars.'

I stared at him.

'Twenty, please.'

Making sure all the car doors were still locked, I quickly checked my wallet. I only had five dollars.

'Is there a problem?'

I held up my EFTPOS card.

'Sorry, I don't have the equipment. You have to pay in cash.'

'I can't,' I whispered.

'How come?'

'I only have this,' I said, showing my five-dollar note.

He looked back at me for a minute, and then gave a little chuckle. All of a sudden, the boom was raised. My path was clear.

'I guess the big corporation that owns this place isn't going to notice if one person doesn't pay.'

'What?'

'Go on,' he grinned, 'get out of here!'

I wound my car window right down and extended my hand out towards him.

We shook hands.

'Thank you,' I said.

I flew out of that car park, with tears of relief and happiness falling down my face. I felt freer than I had for a very long time. I had confronted danger, again, and survived. In fact, the danger had simply melted away. The man hadn't been the threat I'd expected him to be. He was on my side, against the corporation he worked for! I had been frightened, but had managed, this time, not to become paralysed. I drove through the streets, keeping my window all the way down. The rain splashed against my face and against my right arm, but I didn't care. I was back in charge of my life again. I had battled fear, and won.

Once home, I dashed inside to find my mother propped up in bed, reading.

'Do you want a peppermint tea?' I asked.

She looked surprised but nodded.

I brought back two cups and sat down on her bed.

'Kate, I've decided that I'm going back to my course,' I announced. 'I want to finish it.'

'That's good.'

'Yes, I'm thinking that afterwards I might look for a job working with women who've been subjected to violence. I know that my experience was miniscule in comparison to most, and that I've still got a lot to learn, but it's an area that interests me.'

'It was more than enough experience for my liking,' my mother said, sipping her tea. 'And are you planning to move back to your flat?'

'You want me out?'

'Of course not. You know perfectly well that you can stay here for as long as you like.'

'So why the pressure?'

'There's no pressure. I'm only asking because I have my own life to lead. I'm well aware that you don't like my boyfriend but he can't stay away indefinitely.'

I could hardly believe that my own mother was throwing me out of her house, and choosing her boyfriend over me.

'I'll go home tomorrow. Clearly that's what you want.'

'No, darling, I want you to leave when you're ready.'

'Sure.'

She grabbed me by the hand and looked intently into my face. 'So do you think you're ready?'

I hesitated for a moment. Surely if I was going back to TAFE, didn't it make sense to return home as well? But was I ready? Suddenly, I realised that I was. I nodded.

'If you'd like,' Kate continued, 'you can take the green lounge chair in the sunroom. Do you want it?'

'That would be terrific.'

'And you're welcome to take my spare iron too.'

'To iron jeans and t-shirts? No way! And don't even think about packing me off with one of your ancient cookery books.'

Why did my mother always assume that I was just like her? Ever since I moved out, she'd tried to load me up with domestic appliances and recipes.

I got up off the bed and walked out of the room, shutting the door behind me.

'Hey!' she called.

'What is it?' I asked, going back in.

'Karma, please don't close the door.'

I stood there, furious. Why had she deliberately used that name when she knows how much I hate it? Why is it that we both seem to be locked into some kind of power struggle, even though neither of us ever wins? However, my mother's voice cut across my thoughts.

'I'm sorry,' she said. 'I'm well aware that you dislike the name Karma. It's just that I see you as my little baby girl, which is completely ridiculous, I know. You're an adult who is making her own way in the world, and I need to respect that you have chosen a different name. I will try to do better in the future, Jess.'

I was momentarily speechless. This was the first time she had ever used that name. Finally I nodded.

'Thank you, Mum,' I said. 'I'd really appreciate that. And in return, I'll do my utmost to not do anything that annoys you.'

We wished each other goodnight and this time, when I left the room, I left the door wide open.

The very next day I returned home to my flat.

'Where did this come from?' Nikki asked, admiring my new chair.

'My mother gave it to me.'

'Nice!' she said, as she flopped down into it. 'So have they caught that bastard with the knife yet?'

'No, and I don't think they ever will.'

'What? Why the hell not?'

'According to the police, there's not enough information to go on. And frankly, I don't think they're particularly interested in chasing it up. Did I tell you that they asked me what I was wearing at the time?'

'You're kidding me.'

'Yes, as if I was somehow responsible for the attack!'

'That's such bullshit!'

'Absolutely. At least I've managed to put enough pressure on the TAFE director so that he's finally agreed to conduct a review into the safety of women on campus. I know that it's not a big step forward, but it's better than nothing.'

Nikki didn't look convinced.

'Anyway, I'm just trying to get on with my life.'

'Sounds like a plan to me.'

'You know, Nikki, I wish I had a career like you do.'

'A career? Is that what you call it? I love cars, that's all. So of course I want a job where I get to work on them. It's not that complicated.'

'Yes, but I don't have a passion for anything. I did a book-keeping course simply because it was the direct opposite to anything that my parents wanted me to do, not because I loved accounting.'

'Come on, is there anyone in the world who loves accounting?'

'True. And now I'm doing a course in Community Development, and while I have a few ideas about the sort of job I might want at the end, I'm still not 100% certain about any of it.'

'That's okay. Why do you need to be certain right now? Jess, you're smart. You'll figure it out eventually . . . or maybe you will wind up doing a range of different things. Anyway, I think it's time for your present.'

Nikki reached down and pulled a strange black box out of her bag.

'But it's not my birthday.'

'I must have missed the memo that said presents should only be given on birthdays.'

I examined the case.

'It's a machine gun?'

'In your hands,' she grinned, 'it probably will turn into some kind of weapon.'

I opened the lock, to find a pool cue.

'Look, I got it engraved! And it's super easy to slot together. What do you think?' Nikki's face was beaming.

'I don't understand. You said that you're never going to play against me again.'

'I'm not. This is to help you beat someone else. Not me.'

'So you think that I need help?'

She pretended to whack my arm.

'Fine,' I said, 'but who am I going to play?'

'That's your problem.' Nikki shrugged her shoulders. 'I just gave you the cue.'

'Why don't you and I play as partners in a game of doubles?'

'Sure. When?'

'What about now?'

'But is The Purple Crush still open?'

'Let's go somewhere different. What about the local pub?'

'Yeah, why not?'

However, when we arrived at the hotel, we had difficulty in actually getting inside. The place was completely packed. Eventually we managed to squeeze our way through the crush of people, to hover around a pool table. As we waited for our turn, we surveyed the competition. A couple of balding old men were beginning to play two women.

'Come on, sweetheart,' one of them said, sucking in his beer gut and winking at the younger woman. 'Set 'em up. We'll show you how it's done.'

'Pass me a bucket,' groaned Nikki.

'I hope we get to play him,' I whispered back.

'It'd be a pleasure.'

We watched the game carefully. The guys were full of bravado but devoid of any skill. They whacked the ball so hard that one even went over the side of the table, and in fact, they were lucky that any of them made it into a pocket. Didn't they realise that pool is a game of strategy rather than strength? In the end they lost, rather than the women won.

'Bloody dogs!' grinned Nikki. 'That'll teach them.'

'I thought that you liked dogs.'

'Not these ones, I don't!'

'Then back to their kennel they go.'

'Caves, more like it!'

The men crawled away into the crowd, while the victors took on a new pair, this time a man and a woman.

'Hey, Mum, do you want to break?' we heard the younger victor say.

'That's mother and daughter?' I wondered aloud.

'Must be. She doesn't look old enough to be that girl's mother.'

'Maybe she's not her real mother,' I said, with a wink.

Nikki in reply just rolled her eyes. I watched the pairs closely, knowing that it was going to be our turn to play the winners of that game.

The women played reasonably well and both had a good technique. But the mother clearly was an old hand and knew which balls to shoot, whereas the daughter was haphazard in her selection. Why didn't the mother advise her? The daughter was letting the side down.

The couple was also missing some easy shots, basically because they weren't fully concentrating. In between turns, he was drinking his beer when he should have been working out which ball to sink next, while the girl kept examining her nails. She had the sort of hands that could easily feature in a manicure ad, with long pointy nails that were painted bright red.

I fluttered my hands in front of Nikki's face and then glanced in the woman's direction. Nikki instantly caught on.

'With nails like that I'd never need to look for a screwdriver again,' she chuckled.

We turned back to the game. The couple were winning, but only just. All of a sudden, I realised what the problem was and elbowed Nikki in the ribs.

'Now, listen, given that this is the first time we've played together, it's important to—' I whispered.

'Nah, we played once before, against Amanda and Daniel. Remember? We lost.'

'This game is going to be different. You and I need to focus on playing well with each other.'

Nikki looked puzzled.

'Do you want to win?' I asked.

'Absolutely.'

'Then we need to operate as a team.'

'Okay.'

I took my new pool cue out of its case, screwed it together and chalked it thoroughly while we waited. In my hands, my cue felt great – nice and heavy – the way a good pool cue should feel.

Finally, as expected, the couple won and it was our turn to play against them. Nikki hit first and pocketed a ball straight away. Unfortunately, however, the men from the previous game reappeared.

'Good shot. Well done, girlie,' one of them said. 'Now try for that ball over there.'

Nikki went for a different ball, but missed. I groaned inwardly. Those bastards were going to distract her and it was going to be left all up to me. The other side sank two before it was my turn. I pocketed the three obvious balls that were in easy reach, without much effort. Then I stopped and leant on my cue, studying the table.

'Very tricky, I agree,' said someone, coming up beside me. 'What about trying this one?'

I stepped away from him and realised that there was no clear shot for any of the balls. They were all too close to one another. I looked across at Nikki. She grinned back. I examined the layout of the balls again, and in an instant, knew how to set them up for her. I took aim, and hit. One ball ricocheted into a second of our balls, and then hit a third that in turn moved a fourth. Perfect. None, of course, had fallen into a pocket.

'Bad luck, honey,' smirked the guys.

The painted-nail girl was not a good player. She was way off the mark on her ball, but luckily left all of ours where they lay. Her partner scowled at her. I gave the thumbs-up sign to Nikki. She bent down to shoot the ball closest to the left pocket.

'Hang on a minute,' I quickly said.

'What?'

'Just look at the table. Take your time.'

She glanced at my face, studied the balls and then turned back to me.

'That one first?'

I nodded.

Nikki pocketed the first ball I'd set up, then the second, third and fourth, before she spun around to wink at me. I felt so proud of her, and so proud of us.

The game was quickly over. When we potted the black, the table was still littered with their balls. Nikki and I began to sing 'We Are the Champions' at the tops of our voices. The pair we were meant to play next had melted away, but I no longer cared. Nikki and I had won, together.

NOT THE END

To celebrate, Nikki and Jess fronted up to the bar.

'The usual?' asked Jess.

'You know what?' said Nikki. 'Now that you've given up the cigarettes, I reckon that it's my turn to stop drinking Coke. I'm going to have a water.'

'Water? Are you feeling all right?'

'When I start drinking peppermint tea like your mother, you'll know it's time to call an ambulance.'

Nikki and Jess picked up their drinks and made their way through a stream of people who were heading towards the exit. They sat down at one of the many spare tables.

'What a win!'

'We're a great team!'

'Here's to us!'

They clinked glasses, grinning at one another.

'So what happens next?'

'Wouldn't have a clue.'

'Do you reckon that Daniel is going to dump me?'

'Isn't it also possible that you might get sick of him first, and dump him?'

'Yeah, maybe I'll wind up being the dumper rather than the dumpee!'

'Do you want to know what worries me? It's the thought that I'm going to run into another guy with a knife.'

Jess and Nikki gazed at each other for a few moments.

'I'd like to tell you that's never going to happen again, but I can't. There's always going to be arseholes in this world.'

'You're right. I guess it's a matter of dealing with them the best we can.'

Suddenly the music that was blaring out over the hotel's sound system stopped and there was silence.

'Hey, you girls over there,' the bartender called. 'The pub is now closed.'

Nikki and Jess turned around, to find that the place had emptied and that they were the only ones remaining.

'I wish that I could see into the future. Wouldn't it be great if you could fast-forward your life, like on a video tape, to see how it all ends?'

'You want to see how you die?'

'Oh. Good point.'

'Anyway, there can't be a video because we're still making up our lives as we go along. There's no script that we're following. We're the ones calling the shots and there's nobody telling us what to do.'

'Girls!' yelled the bartender. 'You have to leave! Immediately!'

The pair burst out laughing.

'OUT!'

'Okay, okay! We're going!'

Jess and Nikki strode across the room and flung open the door. They linked arms, before walking off down the street. Together, they vanished into the night.